Mountain Cabin

To Mary and Gerald:
who were always there when my
dreams were fulfilled.

by

Harley Herrald

Published and Distributed by:

Granite Publishing and Distribution, LLC
868 North 1430 West
Orem, UT 84057
(801) 229-9023

ISBN: 1-890558-98-2

Library of Congress Catalog Card Number: 00-105816
Printed in the United States of America

Typeset by Myrna Varga, The Office Connection – Orem, Utah
Cover Design by Tammie Ingram
Cover Art by Janette Chandler

Chapter 1

If there is anything more lonely than sitting on the side of a mountain looking down into a valley at a snug cabin, with a thin spiral of smoke rising from its chimney, I guess I don't know what it would be. I sat there by my small fire and watched as a man came from the barn and stopped by the well. After drawing a bucket of water he stopped at the back door and washed up before entering the cabin. It was then I realized how truly lonely I was.

I was broke, out of work, no prospects and at least three hundred miles from anyone I could rightly call friend. I had heard about the big money being made in the mines in Colorado and ridden up from the panhandle country to try my luck. It took me two weeks and most of my money to find out I was not a prospector. I hired on at a silver mine in Leadville and it took me less than a shift to find out I was not an underground miner. I drew my time, all three dollars of it, bought me a sack of flour, a little bait of coffee and headed south. That's how I came to be sitting where I was. No where to go; to or from.

I sat there at the fire for a few minutes listening to my empty stomach complain. As I turned in, I could see the pale autumn sun slide behind the high peaks, which were already lightly dusted with an early snow. I had just about arranged my bedroll to my satisfaction when I heard a blood-curdling scream. It sounded as if it came from across the valley, directly across from my camp. I was sitting bolt upright before I realized it must be a mountain lion. I had been told their scream was much like a woman's. I relaxed then and started to lay back down when another scream echoed across the valley. It was not a mountain lion.

I looked again across the canyon to see a figure dart out from the tree line and start a headlong dash toward the cabin. I could tell the terrain sloped toward the cabin by the way the person was running. It was that sort of out of control movement you see only when someone is running hard, downhill. From the corner of my eye I saw the man come out of the cabin then dash back inside to emerge again with what appeared to be a rifle.

I turned my attention back to the running figure and then I saw why she had screamed. There was a large bear rumbling across the meadow in pursuit. The figure looked back and seemed to quicken the pace of an already head-long flight. The man from the cabin ran about fifty yards toward the beast then knelt and fired. The bear stopped, raised up on its back legs and roared something fierce. Then it took a couple of awkward steps and dropped back on all fours continuing its pursuit. She had gained twenty-five or thirty yards on the bear and as she approached the man he waved her on by while he knelt once again and fired twice more. It was plain to see he scored with only one shot. I wondered why he did not fire again. I was watching the bear to see if the one shot would stop its charge. I glanced back at the man and could tell he must have somehow jammed his weapon. He was frantically trying to work the lever as the bear charged. As the bear closed with the man, I grabbed my rifle and jumped on my horse. Holding a handful of mane, I jerked the picket pin free. It was difficult to stay on as we charged down the mountainside dodging rocks and trees. Luckily I always slept in moccasins for I had given no thought to my boots, let alone a saddle for my horse.

As we broke out on the flat my pony caught either sight or scent of that bear and immediately became almost impossible to control. Even from where I was, I could see the man was in serious trouble. His upper body was completely red with blood. For a moment I hoped it was the bear's, but that thought vanished when I saw the man being shaken from side to side by that bear. About the time I came in range my horse became unmanageable. I slipped to the ground still holding the rope which held the picket pin. I quickly wrapped the pin rope around my arm and hand. The bear suddenly became aware of me and my horse and turned, raised up on its hind legs and roared once again. I had stopped in a small swale from which the bear seemed sky-lighted as it stood. I shot that monster three times right under its chin just as fast as I could work the lever of my rifle. It fell over backwards. I quickly reloaded and scrambled up over the edge of that depression to find both the animal and the man, quite dead.

The man was badly torn up and the bear's chest and front paws were covered with blood. I heard a commotion and turned to see two women running from the cabin. Both carried rifles. It was not until they had almost reached me that I stood, and moving toward them, stopped their approach.

I suggested they might want me to take care of the man. The one shook off my hand angrily. Dashing past, she knelt and, cradling his head in her lap, began to wipe the blood from his still face with her apron. The other woman stood absolutely still with great tears streaming down her cheeks. She did not utter a sound. Her face was distorted with the pain of the scene and tears dripped from her cheeks down off her chin as if they were rain drops. She made not a sound.

I stood, struck dumb by the horror of that instant. I didn't know whether the man was husband to one and father to the other or maybe father to both. I simply did not know enough to comment. So, I turned and quieted my horse, resetting the picket pin to allow him to graze and calm down even though he was still skittish of the dead bear.

When I turned, the one woman was standing beside the other while the second still knelt beside the man, cleaning his face. That the man was dead was immediately obvious. His mutilation denied any hope. It was that torn body that finally prodded me into action. I walked to the woman who knelt and physically lifted her to a standing position.

"Please, Ma'am," I began, "you folks go on back to the cabin. I will clean him up and bring him in when he's fit to be laid out."

She looked at me as if I were a rock or some other object then silently turned and arm in arm the two women trudged back into the cabin.

I went to the well for water and taking two towels from the backdoor wash stand, I returned to the grisly task I had assigned myself. It was long after dark before I carried the amazingly light body to the cabin where I was met by the woman who so silently had wept. She directed me to a sparsely furnished, but spotlessly clean bedroom. There I placed the body on a bed obviously remade just for the final sleep of the man.

I stood there flanked on the one side by the bed, with its silent occupant, and on the other by what I could now see was the younger of the two women. She stood at the foot of the bed grasping its rail while, once again, great tears coursed her face. The other woman came in with a folded quilt with which she carefully covered the body, leaving only the torn face exposed. She then turned, looking me straight in the eye.

"Can you use a hammer and saw?" She bluntly demanded.

Somehow her blunt inquiry required an immediate answer. "Yes, ma'am, I was raised to know both."

"Then, would you be kind enough, come morning, to build a coffin for my husband. You will find tools in the barn. There, also, you will find sawn lumber my husband had prepared for other use but which should do well, the task at hand."

"Yes, Ma'am," I answered, turning my hat in my hands. "Ma'am, I have a camp up on the side of the mountain; I'll go back up there and be down at first light. Ma'am, I'm sure sorry. I wish I could have been faster. Things might have been different."

"Sir," she said, again turning to look me straight into my eyes, "it is of no value to consider what might have been. It is sufficient to deal with the here and now."

"There, old son," I thought, as I turned to leave the room, "is a stronger lady than you've seen in some time."

I edged past the other woman, still standing at the foot of the bed. As I left the house, I thought about the lack of attention I received as I left. There were no good-byes or "We'll see you in the morning." I guess I was impressed by the direct and uncluttered manner these women were accepting their tragedy. For tragedy, it was indeed. Two women left alone in a high mountain valley with winter and snow due within days; weeks on the outside.

It was long into the night before I closed my eyes. I hated the thought of the two of them alone but I couldn't readily understand my feeling of obligation. I owed them nothing, and even if I did; I had no way to settle such a debt, should such even exist. I could neither understand nor dismiss my feelings that cold night.

Chapter 2

I rode down off the mountain in the cold, false dawn of that next day. Night was not yet ready to release its hold and day no more ready to claim the world. As early as it was, I could see smoke rising from the cabin chimney.

The door opened as I walked up and the younger woman, now more composed, stood framed in the soft lamplight.

"Please wash your hands and clean your boots, breakfast will soon be ready."

I could not have been more shocked if she had said the world was ending. Her tone and manner were as if I came to that door daily and this morning was no different than others.

Having cleaned my hands, face and boots and even dusted my hat and clothes, I knocked, to have the door opened almost immediately. Again, by the younger woman. I walked into the kitchen area to a table set with only one plate. The plate was heaped with food; but there was only one plate. As the older woman placed a pan of hot biscuits on the table, she turned to me; "Sir, you will be kind enough to understand that my sister and I will not be eating this morning. Please help yourself and enjoy your food. I ask only that you give thanks to the Lord for your breakfast and that as soon as you have eaten your fill, you attend to the chore you agreed to last evening. Now, if you will excuse my sister and I, we have chores."

Without further ado, each woman picked up a milk bucket and they then quietly let themselves out into the dawn chill. I stood a moment, not really sure what I wanted to do next. My appetite finally won and I seated myself in the single chair drawn to the table. The remaining chairs were propped against the far kitchen wall. I sat there, not sure of what came next. I had heard my father say grace before every meal I had ever taken at my mother's table, but I had never done so since leaving home. Again my appetite won and after a short prayer I fell to the task of demolishing that plate. Admitting I was hungry; that was still some of the best food I had ever eaten, not even excepting my own mother's cooking.

I had just put on my hat and was headed for the door when the women returned. Both were heavily laden with full milk pails and aprons gathered around eggs. I reached to take the pail from the younger woman.

"Thank you, Sir, but I believe you have your own work to do."

To that I had no response, so I stepped around both and headed for the barn. I found the man's tools to be of a decent quality and in excellent condition. I had some difficulty finding the lumber until I removed a tarp covering the boards. Lying atop the boards was a partially finished baby's crib. Also atop the pile were neat sketches of the crib, also drawings for a four-poster bed and a smaller bed. There was plenty of lumber, more than enough to build a coffin and complete the furniture shown in the drawings. I was surprised to find, as I began to build the box, the lumber was good grained cedar.

I was nearing completion of the coffin when the older woman came into the barn with a pitcher of milk and two left over biscuits covered with butter and honey.

"My husband always enjoyed a snack about this time of day." She said by way of a greeting.

So saying, she stopped in mid-stride, and for the first time since the man's death, I believe, she cried. She handed me the pitcher and plate of biscuits then turned to a stanchion post and placing her head and hands against the timber her body was wracked with deep terrible sobs for two or three minutes. I knew not what to say or do. I felt it wiser not to speak to or touch her. So, I stood until she wiped her face and eyes then, visibly composing herself, she turned back to face me.

"Sir, I apologize for the discomfort my grief must cause you. I do hope you will understand."

"Ma'am, the one thing I do understand is the strength you and your sister seem to have in this terrible time. I am honored to be in your presence and will do what I can to ease your load."

I hadn't put that much emotion into what I had to say since I asked Pa for my first pistol. She seemed not to mind, she just smiled faintly.

"Forgive me, sir, you have been so kind and I don't even know your name, nor you ours. My husband is, or was, Jethro Bailey. I am Clatilda and my sister is Jennifer. And, you, sir?"

I jerked my hat from my head, only then realizing my rudeness in not having removed it when she first entered the barn. "My name is Will, ma'am, Will Jackson. I'm from down south of Amarillo way, ma'am. I've lately been prospecting up around Leadville, but I found that not to my liking so I'm headed south to find work."

"From what you have done this morning, you should have no trouble. You seem to do good work, and obviously, you work steady."

"Well, thank you ma'am. I was about ready to come up to the house to get your husband's birth date. I thought to carve it on one of those good cedar boards as a marker."

"How kind of you, Mr. Jackson! I have given you his name, and he was born April 22, 1851. You know the date of his death."

I had finished the coffin and lettered the board for carving when Miss Jennifer came to the barn to summon me to eat. When I walked out of the barn, I was surprised to see the mountains to the west of the valley completely obscured by low clouds. I'd not spent much time in snow country but I recognized snow clouds.

"When did that storm blow in, Miss Jennifer?" I asked.

"Oh, the clouds began gathering shortly after daybreak." She answered. "I'm surprised you didn't notice when you went to the barn this morning."

While I was eating my meal of stew and fresh bread, I glanced out of the only glass window in the cabin to see light snow swirling around under the eaves. Turning to Mrs. Bailey, I put down my spoon and pushed away from the table. "Ma'am, I don't know what your plans are, or if you might be wanting to wait for kinfolk before you bury your husband. But if I don't get at digging your husband's grave it might not be possible, should this storm last or come a hard freeze. So I'll be after digging Mr. Bailey's grave if you'll tell me where you will want it placed."

"Mr. Jackson," Clatilda answered, "as much as I hate to see a man work in weather such as this, I will be obliged if you would do just that. I will see Jethro buried on that little knoll where he was killed. If you could harness the team that's in the barn, I believe they would allow themselves to be used to drag the bear's carcass away, possibly to the edge of that grove of quakies. While you move the bear and dig the grave, Jennifer and I will line the coffin and prepare Mr. Bailey for burial." She said this as calmly as a jigger-boss telling off his crew with the day's work.

After I put on my hat and coat, I walked out into a storm that had all the earmarks of a real humdinger. The wind was howling down off the mountains, swirling the snow as it switched directions every minute or so. I don't know how fast the snow was coming down, but when I had harnessed the team and led them out of the barn, my tracks from the cabin were gone, covered or blown away. Maybe both.

Mrs. Bailey was right, the team gave me no trouble moving the bear's carcass. It was near dark, however, before I finished the grave. I returned to the barn to find both women seated next to the open coffin. I was surprised to see the coffin now held Mr. Bailey's body. How those two ladies did it, I didn't even ask. I loaded the coffin in the back of a spring wagon and headed back to the knoll with the two women marching steadily behind.

I had set some rope and posts across the grave in such a way that allowed me to lower the coffin by myself. When I had placed the coffin, ready to be lowered, I asked Mrs. Bailey if she wanted to say anything.

"No, Mr. Jackson, Jennifer and I have said our good-byes and prayers. It is now time to get on with what is left to do."

I made no comment, but to myself. I was more convinced than ever that I was in the presence of a type of courage and strength I had never before been privileged to be near. I carefully lowered the coffin, and as was the custom, both women tossed a handful of dirt upon its top. By then it was snowing quite hard and there were six or eight inches on the ground. I suggested to the ladies they might want to return to the cabin while I finished the burial. It was then that Mrs. Bailey made a strange request.

"Mr. Jackson," she said, as both women remained by the grave, "have you the power to bless my husband's grave?"

I stopped with a shovel of dirt in mid-air. "Ma'am, I don't know what you mean."

"That will be all right, Mr. Jackson. Just never mind that I asked," she said as she and Jennifer turned and, bucking a strong wind, headed back to the cabin.

It was nearly midnight by the time I replaced the team in their stalls and hung the harness. I turned to see Mrs. Bailey standing at the barn door, pulling a great shawl around her shoulders and carrying a lantern.

"Mr. Jackson," she said, "as soon as you have washed, we have your supper ready."

"Well, I appreciate that, Mrs. Bailey, but I wouldn't want to bother you folks this night; most particularly as late as it is."

"Sir, the food is on the table and your place is set. My sister and I have not eaten since midday yesterday. Please do not keep us waiting." So saying, she turned and stepped out into what had become a howling blizzard.

To be right honest, I'd have been real disappointed had she not insisted. The afternoon, and night's work had created a great emptiness between my shirt collar and belt buckle. I did not fancy trying to go to sleep, as hungry as I was at that moment.

The meal was eaten mostly in silence. Once or twice Mrs. Bailey commented on the weather, and Jennifer thanked me for the job I had done on the coffin. Mrs. Bailey served me a piece of pie and a large cup of milk to finish the meal. I would really have enjoyed a hot cup of coffee, but I saw none, not even a pot. I assumed it to be a luxury they couldn't afford.

As I was finishing my pie, Mrs. Bailey spoke; "Mr. Jackson, I doubt you will be able to continue on your way for a few days, as these storms have a way of dragging out in this country. You will find a comfortable room in the southeast corner of the barn. Mr. Bailey built it to accommodate the occasional visitor and for a hired hand we need and thought to be able to afford next spring. Please use it as you will. Of course you are welcome at our table as long as you are our guest."

Her invitation had a finality that indicated three facts: I would be staying until the storm was over, supper was already over and it was expected I would soon retire to that room in the barn.

I was pleasantly surprised by the room. It was clean, had a good bed and was quite warm, considering its location, the storm and the absence of a stove.

Chapter 3

Daylight found me up, having already tended to the horses, I had begun milking the first of two milk cows the Baileys kept. I had my back to the barn door and my head stuck in that Jersey's flank, deep in thought of better times on my father's ranch. When Mrs. Bailey spoke to me, I almost jumped out of my socks.

"You may not be a miner, and you dress like a cowboy, but I dare say, Mr. Jackson, you've milked a cow or two along the way."

"Yes, ma'am, it was always my chore when a boy."

"Well here's another clean bucket. When you have finished, come to the house. Breakfast will be ready when you are."

How that woman knew I had hoped to complete the milking without interference, I'll never know. I enjoyed that early morning in the Bailey barn as I have few, before or since. Outside, the storm was less intense than it had been the night before, but the snow was still coming down. When I had finished the milking and turned the calves in with their momma's, I headed for the house.

I knocked at the door and was admitted into a warm kitchen which smelled strongly of fresh bread dough. Several loaves were on a table beside the stove, set to rise before baking.

Breakfast was, again, a quiet meal. Mrs. Bailey was quite composed, but Jennifer's face was puffy from weeping.

"Mrs. Bailey," I asked as the meal was over, "Do you folks have any livestock, other than that which you keep in the barn?"

"Yes, Mr. Jackson, and I am worried. Mr. Bailey had gathered our cattle into a pasture in the south end of the valley. The hay he had stacked is all under separate fence, and I am concerned now that the cattle are no longer able to graze. I'm sure there must be at least sixteen or eighteen inches on the level and its been snowing harder since daylight."

"How many head do you have?" I asked.

"My husband told me he had tallied a few over one hundred including three late calves."

"Have you enough hay to feed that many?" I asked. "It would seem a real job for one man to put up enough hay for that much stock."

"Oh yes, my husband said we could feed them through, even if we had an early closed winter; which, it appears, is exactly what we may have. But now, I'm worried that hay may not be of much use."

"Mrs. Bailey, can you tell me about the lower end of this valley? Are there any major landmarks; like rocks, trees or streams?"

"I don't believe I know what you mean, Mr. Jackson. Of course, there are rocks, trees and two streams both of which run north to south."

"What I mean, ma'am, is that if I went down there in this snow are there markings, or such, I could use so as not to get lost?"

"Oh of course, Mr. Jackson. My husband transplanted cedar trees for the past three years. There is a straight line of cedars, one every hundred feet or so, all the way to the south pasture gate."

"You mean the pastures are fenced?"

"Surely! My husband fenced our entire ranch, except for the strip down from the west side of our valley to the forest on the east. It is in this strip that our home and barn are placed. He left this open to allow free movement for ourselves and travelers such as yourself."

"It would seem your husband was a planning man."

"Of a certainty, Mr. Jackson! He had already purchased the nails and cut and peeled the logs he intended to use in building an addition to our home next spring."

"Ma'am, you mean that if I head due south and follow a line of cedar trees I could reach those cattle?"

"Oh, yes, Mr. Jackson. My husband planted those trees for just that purpose in the event of a storm such as this."

"That settles it then. As soon as I can saddle my pony, I'll go see about your cattle."

I was leading my pony out of the barn when Jennifer came with a package. "Clatilda sent this. It is food for your noon meal in case you don't get back until late."

Before I rode away from the barn, I checked to make sure of the wind direction. It was, and if the drifts were any indication had been for some time, blowing out of the west. Putting the wind on my right shoulder, I headed south.

It was remarkably easy to follow the line of cedar trees. I had expected small, three or four-foot high bushes. Instead most were well over six feet tall. I wondered at the job it had been to find and transplant that many six foot cedars. I was once again impressed with the work of Jethro Bailey.

Even with the trees to guide me, it took almost two hours for my horse to fight through the snow and pull up in front of a gate. I found what I believed to be all of the cattle, pushed up against a line of old cottonwoods stretched along a good sized stream. They were within sight of three large hay stacks. But, as Mrs. Bailey had said, these stacks were all under separate fence. The only thing those dumb beasts could do was stand at the fence and bawl. I opened the wire gate and choused that herd into the first stack. It was only then I realized each of the three stacks was under separate fence.

I saw some suspicious mounds to the west and when I rode over I found another half-dozen hay stacks. Someone had been busy that summer. To cut and stack that much hay told me that Jethro Bailey worked twenty-four hours every day or was four or five men. I rode back and secured the wire gate in an open position then rode among the cattle in order to better check their condition. I located the three new calves and as nearly as I was able to tally in the storm, I found one hundred and eight head. If that wasn't all of the Bailey herd, it was going to have to do.

By the time I started back along that line of cedar trees, I knew I was in trouble. My feet were numb and my hands were almost without feeling. I had been in the saddle for over four hours. What was worse, the wind had shifted and was now blowing first from the north and then from the northeast. I was frequently disoriented and much afraid I would lose that line of trees. What made things worse was it was snowing harder and the trees were becoming more like mounds of snow than separate objects.

It was full dark before I noticed my horse had quickened his pace and I was more aware of the wind change than noticing the bulk of the barn. My pony stopped, and I reached out to feel the structure. It took several attempts for me to open the barn door. My hands were then in such a condition I was unable to unsaddle my horse and left him standing in the stall while I made for the house. I had taken a few steps before I realized the danger I faced. I turned back into the barn and fumbled with several hanks of rope hung by the tack room. I managed to join them together into a single strand I believed to be long enough to reach the cabin. I looped and tied one end around a stall stanchion and once again set out into the blinding snow. I stumbled into the back of the cabin with little realization I had reached safety.

I tried to open the door, but found it bolted from inside. I beat upon the door with my numbed fist until it was opened to reveal both women confronting me with rifles at the ready. They quickly helped me in to the warmth of the kitchen, and I remember the sudden heat was oppressive and at the same time, comforting. That's the last I remembered until the next morning.

Chapter 4

I awoke in the same bed upon which I had placed Bailey's body. Clatilda was seated in a rocker in the corner quietly working on a piece of lace. She became aware of my gaze and placed the lace in her lap. She then returned my look as directly as you please.

"Mr. Jackson, you do sleep soundly. Are you hungry?"

"Mrs. Bailey, now that you mention it, I am very hungry."

"Then you dress and come into the kitchen. There is food ready."

I was shocked, confused and right embarrassed to see my pants and shirt neatly folded upon the foot board of the bed. I hurriedly dressed and went into the kitchen to find Mrs. Bailey setting a bowl of steaming mush on the table.

"Sit, Mr. Jackson," she said, "I have fresh bread and honey also."

As I ate, she busied herself with what appeared to be the

preparation of pies. She worked quickly and seemed not to waste any motion or ingredients in the pastry she was preparing.

"Where is Miss Jennifer?" I asked.

"Jennifer is in her bed, sir. She is not well this morning."

"I'm sorry," I said, "I hope it's nothing serious."

At that moment we were startled by a knock on the outside door. I started to rise but Mrs. Bailey had turned to the door preceding my motion and waved me to my seat. She opened it to two men and an older boy standing in the deep snow outside the cabin door. It had stopped snowing and the sun could be seen breaking through the thinning clouds.

"Sister Bailey," the older of the men addressed Mrs. Bailey, "we've come to see how you and Jethro weathered the storm."

She invited them in and introduced them to me as Bishop Terry, his brother John Terry and John's son Joseph. She went on to introduce the Bishop as her church leader.

Mrs. Bailey seated her guests and served them milk, bread and honey. Then in total calm and a frighteningly absolute composure she related the events of the past four days. When she was through John Terry asked of Jennifer. Mrs. Bailey told him of Jennifer's condition and he only commented that it was to be expected and hoped she would be well. Mrs. Bailey assured him she prayed this should be.

For some reason, Bishop Terry felt himself to be in control of the situation. He began to advise Mrs. Bailey what she should and should not do about the ranch, livestock and even promising to build the addition to her cabin, come spring. I felt somewhat out of place and rose to excuse myself but Mrs. Bailey made, what I considered at the time, a strange request.

"Mr. Jackson, if you would be so kind, I wish you to stay for a moment."

I sat back down, not knowing what to expect or from whom.

"Mr. Jackson, you have said you were looking for work. Would you be willing to work for me? I will pay you what other ranch hands earn in this area. You may have the room in the barn. I have a stove that can be installed there for heat and you will of course take your meals at my table."

I was very uncomfortable. Her offer of a job was right good news and I intended to accept but I was somehow put off by the almost forbidding presence of the two men also seated at the table. Before I could answer, Bishop Terry spoke.

"Sister Clatilda, I think you will find that we brethren will be quite able to care for you and Sister Jennifer. It might not be proper for you to have a hired man at this time."

"Bishop Terry," Mrs. Bailey began, fixing that gentleman with her direct, intense gaze, "I will thank you not to question the propriety and rightness of my business arrangements. I know you wish only to help, but Mr. Jackson has already shown himself to be an able and willing worker. Thus far he has done more than most would and what he has done he has done well, willingly, and without mention of pay."

Well, I'll tell you, at that point I was about ready to ask for a raise and I didn't even know what the pay was going to be.

"Sister Clatilda," the Bishop said, holding one hand out toward Mrs. Bailey, "please don't be offended. I only thought to care for you and Sister Jennifer. If you wish to hire Mr. Jackson, please do so. You may also expect the men of the ward to continue offering their seasonal assistance. One thing more; may we count on Mr. Jackson to assist us as needed?"

"Surely, Bishop, you know we are at your call, even as Jethro was."

"Mr. Jackson," Bishop Terry said as he stood, "I will be talking to you from time to time. Your new employer is well thought of here and I am sure, in time, so shall you be."

He then stepped around the table and directed his attention to Mrs. Bailey. "I imagine we should visit Brother Bailey's grave site and take care of the blessing, should we not?"

He, his brother and the boy, along with Mrs. Bailey left the house and it was almost an hour before Mrs. Bailey returned, alone.

I had taken the time to replenish the kitchen wood box. This chore I was just completing as she walked into the kitchen.

"Mr. Jackson, you never said if you would accept my offer of employment," she said by way of greeting.

"Ma'am, I've never worked for a woman, but I suspect that if you will allow me to do the outside work as I know it should be done there should be no problems, and I will be grateful to accept your offer."

"Fine, Mr. Jackson. I am told ranch hands in this area receive twenty-five to thirty dollars per month plus room and board. I had thought to offer you forty dollars per month, room and board and to charge you with the responsibility of operating my ranch."

A feeling of rightness came over me that I have never been able to explain, even to myself. I accepted and turned, leaving the house. I had never been emotional about any job I'd ever taken or quit. For some reason, I was right pleased to be working on the Bailey ranch.

Chapter 5

That winter was difficult. It seemed I always had two or three more jobs than I could get done each day. I never really got behind, it just seemed I never got caught up. Mrs. Bailey insisted that an absolute minimum of work be done on Sunday, or the "Sabbath" as she called it. I would save jobs that could be done in the barn on that day. She would rarely come to the barn by that time, except to feed the hens she was carrying through the winter. So it seemed that on Sundays I was busier than ever.

Miss Jennifer was sick all fall hardly leaving her room even for meals. Only once did Mrs. Bailey make any comment of her concern. Christmas Eve Mrs. Bailey came to the barn in mid-afternoon. She asked me to please ride to the Terry place and fetch Mrs. Terry. She added that I was to ask Bishop Terry and his brother to come and to do so quickly.

On the ride back, John Terry made a comment that I thought I had misunderstood. We were loping along behind the Bishop's buggy when he glanced over at me and said something about hoping, "Sister Bailey doesn't lose the baby."

Mrs. Bailey was not very tall but she had sort of a willowy build. I just didn't see how she could be expecting a baby and I not have noticed. But I had never had much to do with ladies except for my mother, so I didn't feel qualified to make any judgments. I confess I did worry some, though, for the rest of the way back home. It seemed Mrs. Bailey had suffered enough without now losing the last thing Mr. Bailey could leave her.

When we arrived back at the ranch, John Terry and I took care of the horses and buggy while the Bishop and his wife went inside for it was coming on to dark and turning cold as only a high mountain valley can on a clear late December evening.

While John and I were caring for the livestock, Bishop and Mrs. Terry disappeared in to the cabin. When we had the horses stabled and as I was forking hay down from the loft, Bishop Terry stuck his head in the barn door and told John to come into the house and to do so immediately.

I didn't really know what to do so I spent the night finishing a cedar table I'd been working on for Mrs. Bailey's kitchen. It was to be her Christmas gift. I was right pleased I had been able to keep it a secret. It was just breaking day and I was setting back, admiring what had turned out to be a right nice piece of furniture, when the Bishop walked into the barn.

"Well, Mr. Jackson, it appears that once again you must be asked to build a coffin for the Bailey family."

My heart jumped into my throat as I asked, "Mrs. Bailey?"

"Yes, Sister Terry was able to save the baby, but not Sister

Jennifer."

I had long since reconciled myself to the plural marriage of Miss Jennifer and Miss Clatilda to Jethro Bailey but somehow the existence of a child placed the situation in sharper focus.

I was just finishing the coffin when Bishop Terry and Miss Clatilda came into the barn carrying quilts with which to line the box.

"Mr. Jackson, it seems you have shared most of the sorrow of this valley. I hope you will stay to see the joy that surely must come," Clatilda said, as greeting.

Not knowing what to say, I turned and removed the lid exposing the interior for lining.

"Have you eaten, Mr. Jackson?" asked Mrs. Terry stepping through the barn door.

"No ma'am, but I'll not have time. There is stock that has needed tending since yesterday. I'll be heading out now to take care of my chores."

"On Christmas morning, Mr. Jackson?" Mrs. Terry said, rather sharply.

"Ma'am those calves know nothing of Christmas morning."

I gathered my rig and headed for the barn corral. As I stepped through the door, I felt someone coming after me. I turned to find Miss Clatilda had followed me out.

"Will, can the animals not fend for themselves this morning? I would be pleased if you could find work to busy yourself around the house this day."

I didn't know what to say. I believe we were both very aware this was the first time she had spoken to me using my given name. It was also the first time she had asked anything of me in such a manner.

"Yes ma'am." I said, turning back into the barn.

I went to the newly finished table and picking it up, carried it into the house and into the kitchen. I then cleared off the old table and took it out to the barn. I am sure all there saw what I did. They made no comment.

I gathered the necessary tools and, as I turned from the wall I asked Miss Clatilda if Miss Jennifer was to be buried beside Mr. Bailey.

"If you please, Mr. Jackson." was all she said. "There" I thought as I left the barn, "is still the strongest lady I've ever seen."

As I rounded the cabin and headed up the hill toward Jethro Bailey's grave site, John Terry came up behind me. "I'll give you a hand with this, Mr. Jackson," he said, "I imagine the ground will be frozen hard for some way below the surface."

I told him I was grateful, for I had not been looking forward to the chore.

It was mid-afternoon by the time we were finished, and we were both worn out. It had all been pick and shovel and not an easy task.

When we returned to the barn we found the Bailey team hitched and the wagon loaded with no small amount. Bishop Terry stepped out of the cabin as if he had been watching for us. He was followed by Mrs. Terry with yet another covered basket and finally, Miss Clatilda carrying a tightly wrapped bundle I assumed to be the baby.

"Mr. Jackson," Miss Clatilda said, "it is necessary we take the baby into the settlement. He will not accept cows' milk, and we hope to find a wet-nurse in town."

"Yes ma'am, I'll take care of everything until you get back," I said.

"And Miss Jennifer?" I asked.

"She is in the house which, by now, is quite cold. I will be back in two or three days. We will complete that chore then. But for now, the baby must be my first consideration."

So saying, she handed the baby up to Mrs. Terry, then stepped up into the wagon, regaining possession of the child.

Bishop Terry slapped the reins smartly and soon the wagon was a disappearing dot in the distance.

I stood there beside the barn door feeling more alone than I had in these past three months. I had no real contact with Miss Jennifer, but I had seen Miss Clatilda two, sometimes three or four times each day. I now faced up to a week alone. "Well now," I thought, "maybe I can get caught up on some of my work."

I finally went back into the barn as darkness settled in the valley. When I lit my lamp, I found three fresh loafs of bread wrapped in a dish towel sitting on the cold stove. There was also a plate of freshly sliced elk along with a bowl of boiled potatoes. Leave it up to Mrs. Bailey to see everything was in order.

For the next few days, I worked hard and got much done. However, the ranch was a lonely place made less comfortable by the presence of Miss Jennifer's body in the cabin. I was never one to be concerned by ghosts or stories like that, but it was not a comfortable time.

It was on New Year's day that I found Bishop Terry's big springboard wagon standing by the barn when I returned from letting the cattle into another of Jethro Bailey's hay stacks. As I stepped down from my horse, Mrs. Terry opened the door and called for me to come into the cabin.

I walked in to find Bishop Terry, Mrs. Terry, Miss Clatilda and Miss Jennifer's baby. Obviously someone had been found to feed the baby for it looked to be quite healthy as it lay sleeping in a wicker basket set upon the new cedar table.

"Mr. Jackson, I hope you fared well while we were away," Clatilda greeted me.

"Yes ma'am, and it would appear the baby found a source of nourishment."

"Yes, I'm afraid you'll find that source in the barn."

"In the barn?"

"Yes, Mr. Jackson, we found the baby can tolerate goats' milk. I'm afraid we've added to the livestock you must care for. There are now two goats in addition to everything else that must be fed and milked."

"Well, now, ma'am, that's just fine. I'll have to learn to milk them. I'm afraid I know nothing about goats."

"Come, Mr. Jackson, I'll show you how," Bishop Terry said, slipping into his jacket, "I've been around goats most of my life."

It was then that a panhandle cowboy became a goat herder.

While Bishop Terry was milking the goats, he asked of my family and where I'd lived, and he wanted much detail. He sounded much like an over-protective father. Finally, this line of conversation seemed too much.

"Bishop Terry, I suppose you feel you should check upon me, your being the head of Mrs. Bailey's church and all, but sir, on this ranch, I'm a hired hand. No more. I came from God-fearing folk and have no need to care for anything here but the stock and ranch."

"Mr. Jackson, I did not mean to offend you, but you must understand our people have not had an easy time of it and we are naturally shy of strangers."

"Bishop Terry, let me tell you how it is and will be on the ranch. So far, Mrs. Bailey likes my work and she pays on time and in full. Should either of these two things change, I expect I'll be gone. There's not much else that needs talking about."

"Very well, Mr. Jackson. Should you have need to discuss any problems, I will be at your beck and call sir."

"That's good enough for me."

Bishop Terry returned to the cabin with the goat's milk while I unsaddled my horse and set about my evening chores.

Just before dark I heard the Terry's leave and shortly thereafter Miss Clatilda came out to the barn to tell me supper would be ready in an hour.

"Thanks, ma'am, but I killed me a snowshoe rabbit down in the south pasture this afternoon and roasted it while I watched the cattle settle into the new hay stack."

She looked at me strangely but just said that was fine and she'd see me in the morning.

I slept but little that night. I had a good job, a good boss, and it was the middle of the winter. I spent most of the night trying to figure how to tell Mrs. Bailey I was leaving.

I had the cows and goats milked before daylight that next morning and packed what little I owned on my saddled horse.

I waited at the barn door until Miss Clatilda came out to call me to breakfast. As she stepped out of the cabin, I picked up my pails of milk and walked out of the barn. She looked at me strangely, then wished me a good morning.

"Breakfast is ready, Mr. Jackson and I see you have been early at your chores."

I carried the milk in and set it on a sideboard next to the stove.

"Mr. Jackson, if you will, I would like you to finish closing Miss Jennifer's grave this morning. Bishop Terry and I buried her last evening before you got in but he had to return to the settlement on other business and the darkness prevented me asking you to complete the task last night."

"Yes ma'am, I'll go do it now."

"No, Mr. Jackson, now you must eat. I venture that rabbit is not fit fare for a working man."

I'll swear she knew, if for no other reason than the twinkle in her eye.

I had almost forgotten how good the food was at Clatilda Bailey's table. She told me Bishop Terry had hauled supplies she had purchased while in town with the baby, and she was again able to have that with which to prepare a proper meal. I'd noticed no problem in that area.

She was feeding the baby as I left to close the grave. Cold as it was that morning it was not a chore to which I looked forward with any pleasure. It was mid-morning when I returned to the barn with my tools. I had thought to carve Miss Jennifer a marker, like the one I had made for Mr. Bailey. I put the tools away then went to the cabin to ask about Miss Jennifer's birth date.

It took a few moments for Miss Clatilda to open the door at my knock. She apologized saying she had to put the baby down and cover it so the cold air from the open door would not hit it.

"I'm afraid, Mr. Jackson, I've idled away the morning playing with the boy. I'm way behind in my work."

"I meant to ask you this morning if it was a boy or girl. I forgot. Have you named him yet?"

"Yes, Mr. Jackson, he has been named and blessed by the Elders of my church. The name by which he shall be known to the world is, William Jethro Bailey. The Jethro for his father and the William for Sister Jennifer's father."

"That's a good name, ma'am. How is he to be called?"

"For now, Mr. Jackson, we will call him William."

"He looks to be a healthy young man, Miss Clatilda. You should be proud of him. Ma'am, I came in to find out Miss Jennifer's birth date and to ask if you want to show her date of passing as Christmas day or the twenty-fourth, seeing as how she died in the night on Christmas Eve. It might someday make it easier for little William not to know his mother died on Christmas Day."

"That's very thoughtful, sir, but as you probably do not know, in our faith, we do not view death with the sorrow some do. However, your thoughtful consideration of a child's feelings is good, and I agree. Please show Miss Jennifer's death as occurring on December twenty-fourth."

I carved the marker and had it set in time for a late dinner. Miss Clatilda apologized for the lateness and promised a treat for supper.

I decided to wait until after supper to tell her I was leaving.

I caught Miss Clatilda looking strangely at me several times during supper. I somehow couldn't bring myself to make small talk. I had hoped the baby would be awake to occupy her time and attention, but he slept quietly throughout the meal. When Miss

Clatilda served the pie for dessert, it was with a large dollop of sweet cream on top. Hot apple pie with sweet cream, and I was quitting.

"Mr. Jackson," she said when she had sat down at the table again, "you have seemed quiet this evening and it came to me that I never thanked you for the fine Christmas gift. I hadn't realized how shabby my old table looked until I saw your beautiful gift. Please don't be offended by my thoughtlessness."

"Mrs. Bailey, that was not the reason for my silence. Bishop Terry and I had a talk the other evening and much he said made sense. I believe it will be best if I head on down toward where I came from, and you can get one of your own people to run your ranch. I'll be going—he may send someone out to help until you can find someone permanent."

"Have you given this much consideration, Mr. Jackson?"

"Yes, ma'am, I have, and under the circumstances Bishop Terry is probably right."

"Right about what, Mr. Jackson?"

"Well, ma'am, he seems concerned about me being here and you a woman alone and all."

"Mr. Jackson, do you and Bishop Terry think I should be afraid of you?"

"No ma'am! I don't know about Bishop Terry but as for me I don't think there is much in this world you fear. But, ma'am, yours seems a close-knit group of folks and I'd have no harm, by word or otherwise, come to you because of my presence."

"Mr. Jackson, I was raised to take care of myself and allow others the same freedom. I will not try to dissuade you, but, I will say I regret your decision."

"Yes ma'am. Well, I'll be going at first light. I'll milk and feed the stock first. And, I will stop by Bishop Terry's on my way through the settlement."

"Very well, sir," she said standing to clear the dishes.

I saw that supper and our conversation was over so I went to my room and turned in.

Daybreak saw me standing at the barn door with two pails of cows milk and one of goats milk for little William. Miss Clatilda opened the cabin door almost as soon as I had closed the barn door.

I set the milk inside the door and she handed me a package, warm to the touch, with two twenty-dollar gold pieces on top.

"I thought you might want an early start, Will. So I prepared your breakfast to take with you and eat along the way. The other is your pay with a little extra traveling money."

I didn't know what to say. I just stood there like some great oaf and stared at the package she held out to me.

"Here, Will, take it. I must close the door before William gets cold."

I took the package, slipping the coins into my jacket, and stepped back as she closed the door.

I stood there a moment feeling I was about to make a bad mistake.

But, I had made up my mind so I crossed the yard to my horse and stepped up into the saddle.

Chapter 6

The ride into the settlement was long and cold. It was, I thought, about seven miles. By the time I asked about and located Bishop Terry's house, I was cold, confused and more than somewhat impressed with my stupidity.

When I explained the situation to Bishop Terry, he was surprised and as he said, some disappointed.

"I thought this was what you wanted," I said, more sharply, I guess, than I intended.

"You just don't understand, do you, Mr. Jackson?"

"I don't know what's to understand. You don't like the idea of someone, not of your church, being out to the Bailey place, and I don't feel inclined to argue the point."

"Mr. Jackson, I will not argue with you about this matter or anything else. But, know this, had I been in the least way uncomfortable with your presence on Clatilda Bailey's ranch, you would have been gone before now. I am sorry to see you go, but I wish you well and safe passage to your destination."

I rode out beyond the last building in the little settlement. There was a big grove of cottonwoods along a stream. I stopped there and built a fire and finally ate the, now cold, breakfast Miss Clatilda had made for me.

As I sat in that grove of trees I started to wonder if I was so sure about the move. Why did I feel so bad and why was I putting off leaving this valley?

"Well," I thought, "you've always been honest with yourself. Why not just admit, if only to yourself, what the real reason is for not wanting to leave the country."

Clatilda Bailey, another man's widow! And, for less than six months at that.

"My friend," I thought, "there is simply no chance she will ever have more for you than a good meal and a hard day's work. If, and when, she ever marries again it will be one of the men from her church. You were right in leaving. You should get started for home."

That's when I stood up, kicked out the fire, tightened the saddle cinch, stepped up and headed back to the Bailey ranch.

I rode into the door yard just as full darkness was settling. Miss Clatilda came out of the barn carrying two milk buckets. When she saw me, she stopped, set the buckets on the ground, pulled her shawl up around her head and turned to me.

"Did you leave something here, Mr. Jackson?"

"Yes ma'am, I believe I left my good sense."

She just smiled, reached down and picked up her milk buckets.

"Stable your horse, Mr. Jackson and come on in. We will discuss your good sense over supper."

When I knocked, the cabin door opened immediately. It felt good, stepping into that warm, spotlessly clean, cabin once again.

"Is William doing well?" I asked.

"Yes, Mr. Jackson he sleeps and eats. Which, for now, is his job. He seems quite competent in his work."

"Mrs. Bailey, I have much to say to you, and I don't know where to begin."

"Mr. Jackson, you take off your coat and wash your hands. Possibly I have a few things to say that will make your way easier."

I did not know what to expect, but I did as she asked.

"Mr. Jackson, let me begin by saying how glad I am to see you. Whatever was said between you and Bishop Terry, may or may not be important as far as you and this ranch are concerned. Bishop Terry is a good and a kind man, but he speaks neither for me nor this ranch. You are unaware of the unique position Bishop Terry holds in the lives of those of us who are members of his flock. But, of one thing you may be assured, this is my ranch and I will run it as I see fit. If anything you do or say displeases me, I will tell you so. If either your work or presence on this ranch becomes intolerable, I will tell you to leave. Remember that, Mr. Jackson. I won't ask or simper about like some schoolgirl. I will tell you, flat out."

During this brief conversation she had placed stew, bread and milk on the table. I started to talk but she stopped me.

"Eat, Mr. Jackson, you must be cold and hungry after this day."

Gratefully, I started to eat. It was no use. I felt I had to say what was on my mind and right then.

"Mrs. Bailey, what I have done today was stupid. I'm sorry. I could go on about what Bishop Terry and I discussed but, looking back, I see I probably took it all wrong. Ma'am, I'm an 'out of work cowboy'. I'm looking for work. Will you hire me?"

"On one condition, Mr. Jackson."

"Just name it."

"I will ask you to return the traveling money I gave you this morning and the wages I owed you. I can ill afford to be paying bonuses to those who work for me."

I got up from the table and stepped over where my jacket hung and extracted the two gold coins. These I laid beside her plate.

"Let's just say we are all even, right now, and start from here. Besides, I haven't spent any of the other money you've paid me up to now."

She didn't protest. She simply picked up the money and dropped it into her apron pocket.

"Mr. Jackson," she said as she stood, "I have pie from last night in my warming oven. Would you have it plain or do you want it with cream?"

"Ma'am, I'll take cream, always."

She smiled and once again I wondered why I had ever been so stupid as to leave.

After I'd had my pie, I excused myself and went to my room. She said nothing more other than good night and even that was as if that day had never happened.

Chapter 7

When I walked out of the barn the next morning I saw a rider coming from the direction of the settlement. I had forgotten that I had asked Bishop Terry to send help. Soon, I could see it was John Terry's son, Joseph.

"Hello, Mr. Jackson, Bishop Terry sent me out. He said you had left. He sent me out to help Sister Bailey."

"I'm sorry, John, there's been a mix-up, and I caused it. I don't know if you'll be needed or not. Let's go talk to Miss Clatilda."

I turned to the cabin just as the door opened.

"Good morning, John, I imagine I know why you're here," she said.

"Yes ma'am, Bishop Terry said I was to come work for you and we'd talk more about it on Sunday."

"Well, come in out of the cold, John, and we'll discuss it over breakfast."

John protested that he had already eaten but willingly accepted the filled plate offered him.

Miss Clatilda explained to John that he would not be needed at this time. He seemed more relieved than anything else.

After breakfast, I saddled my pony and went down to the south pasture to check the cattle. I think I might not have noticed anything amiss had I not noted the absence of one of the three early calves. Then I did a more careful tally and found four head of grown stock and the one calf, missing from the original tally I had made the previous fall. To be sure, I counted the herd a second time. The area around the four fenced pastures and the stream were so trampled by the cattle that no strange tracks were evident. I rode back toward the ranch for at least a quarter mile then began a swing to the east in order to encircle the pastures to see if I could pick up any sign of where the cattle may have been driven off. I had no doubt that they had been taken for the fencing put up by Jethro Bailey would not allow otherwise. They might have drifted in the good weather but with the ground covered, as it was, with snow, I was sure they'd not go far from the stacked hay. I circled back south after crossing the stream. I'd gone no more than a few hundred yards when I came upon the tracks of the cattle and at least two shod horses. I sat there for a few minutes trying to decide whether to follow the tracks or return to the barn for my pistol and rifle. I had taken to leaving them in my room since I'd gone to work for the Bailey's. I turned and started for the ranch in a long lope.

I gathered my weapons, an extra catch rope and my heavy coat and slicker. As I was tying my coat and slicker behind my saddle, Miss Clatilda came out of the cabin.

"Mr. Jackson, is there a problem?"

"Yes ma'am. We seem to be missing four head and one of the new calves. I found tracks where they had been driven off. I aim to go get them back."

She asked me to wait a minute and dashed back into the cabin. Moments later she returned with a package she stuffed into my saddlebag.

"There's bread and roast elk, Mr. Jackson, should you be gone longer than you expect."

"Miss Clatilda, the people who stole your cattle might not be too willing to give them up. There may be trouble."

"Are you afraid, Mr. Jackson?"

"No ma'am, I just wanted you to know I intend to bring those cattle back, whatever it takes."

Chapter 8

"Mr. Jackson, I will not have my livestock stolen from me. I would not want you to be injured or killed over cattle. I only ask that you be careful."

"Ma'am, that's a chance I bargained for when I hired on."

"Go carefully, Will," was all she said as she stepped back from my horse.

As I rode away, I wondered where Clatilda Bailey had come from. Wherever it was, they raised their women strong and honest.

When I got back to where the tracks led away from the stream, they were still there, clear and deep. So clear and deep that I was convinced the cattle had to have been stolen within the last day or so.

The tracks went up into the rolling hills and through the pinion trees where they continued southeasterly. No attempt had been made to hide the trail. In fact there were places where the cattle had been driven across open space when they could have easily been kept in the trees. Either my rustlers were stupid or they didn't care if they were followed. I didn't know which bothered me more.

It was coming on dark when I spotted a light toward the end of a long narrowing valley. I'd been riding in for about an hour. At first I couldn't tell whether it was a campfire or a light from a building. Before I could get close enough to identify the light, darkness fell. And although my eyes had grown accustomed to the dark, I was still unable to see the source of the light. I was near stopping and waiting until daylight before I might walk into a mess, when a bright full moon started slipping up over the mountains to the east. In less than an hour that whole area was bathed with a light nearly as bright as day. Then I saw the house and outbuildings down the valley where the light was coming from.

As I rode closer to the buildings, I could see no one other than the animals in the corrals.

I rode up to the larger corral and there were the four head and the calf. The calf was the only animal not carrying the J Bar B brand clearly visible in the moonlight.

There were three horses in the next corral. Two saddle horses and a plow horse. Both of the two saddle horses showed signs of recent hard riding.

I sat there trying to figure out just how to handle the situation when I heard a baby crying. At first I didn't believe what I was hearing, but as the infant continued to wail, there was no denying the sound.

"Great," I thought, "I've got at least two rustlers and now a baby. Most likely, the baby's mother also." All the brief plans I'd made dissolved in the sound of that baby's cry.

Finally I decided to just confront who or whatever I might find in the cabin. I rode my horse to the cabin front and hailed the house. The door opened almost immediately, and there stood a tall slender man silhouetted by the light from the cabin. He demanded, "Who are you, and what do you want?"

"Mister, I'm just riding through and wondered if you'd let me sleep in your barn tonight. It's awful cold, and there's a lot of snow on the ground."

"Who is it, Ray?" I heard a woman ask from behind the man.

"Just some drifter wanting to sleep in the barn, Blanch," the man said over his shoulder.

"Well tell him to come on in and get warm before he goes out there. I'll get him a cup of coffee."

I wanted that coffee almost as bad as I did the cattle.

"Get down and come on in, cowboy," the man said turning away from the open door.

I stepped off my pony and left him ground-hitched right in front of the cabin door.

I walked into a single room building that was oppressively hot. There were three people there plus the baby. Ray, who'd opened the door, a woman holding a still fussing baby and a boy who looked to be about twelve, give or take a year or two.

"Name's Will Jackson," I said to the man who'd turned away from me to a roaring stove upon which sat a bubbling coffee pot.

"We're the Taylors. I'm Blanche. That there's my boy Clendon and you already met my husband, Ray. And this here fuss-budget is our littlest, Janie."

"Here's your coffee, cowboy. Drink up. Don't put your horse in the barn. Put him in with the others in that small corral," Ray said, handing me a chipped blue granite cup.

One sip and I was through with the coffee. I'd had better to drink from a hoofprint where it hadn't rained in weeks.

"Nice looking cows you got, Mr. Taylor," I said warming my hands around the hot cup.

"Yeah, that's the start of my herd when that little bull calf gets bigger, he'll help me get my ranch going."

"That'll take a while. He don't look more than a couple of months old."

"Well, you know how ranching is, Jackson, you get the right stock then just be patient."

"Yeah, and hope you don't have any trouble with rustlers."

"What you mean by that, cowboy?"

"Just what I said, Taylor. Hard work can pay off if the thieves don't get at you."

"You think I'm a thief, cowboy?"

I had transferred the cup to my left hand and unbuttoned my coat. "Yeah, Mr. Taylor, that's just what I think you are. I've trailed those four head and that calf all day right into your corral. Now I'm taking them back where they came from."

"And you think I'm just going to stand here and let you do that. What do you think me and my boy are going to be doing, just standing around while you steal from me?"

"That does it! You, Taylor, get your coat on! I'll leave your boy here to take care of your woman, but, friend, you're coming with me!"

"But Mr. Jackson, we was just trying to get us a start," Blanch Taylor whined, "we heard, before we came out, here lots of big ranchers got their start this way. And Ray told me the herd he took those cows from must have had over a hundred head in it."

"Lady, I don't care what you heard or where you came from. What your husband did is called rustling, and lots of folks have been hanged for doing what he did and most without any trial at all."

"You ain't hanging my Pa, are you?" the boy said, jumping off the bed where he sat.

"Not yet, son. We'll let the sheriff handle that part."

"You ain't got no right to haul me off to some sheriff." Taylor said.

"Man, don't you have any idea what kind of trouble you're in? Friend, consider yourself lucky you're not dead right now. When I came through your door, I was fully prepared to kill you."

"You'd kill my husband over a few dumb beasts? What kind of person are you?"

"Lady, I don't know where you people came from or what kind of folks you have been around, but wherever it was, you lived some different from the way we do in this country. If you think you can go around stealing people's livestock, you'd better head back to where you came from."

I turned back to Taylor as the cabin was filled with a roar. I felt myself slammed back into the closed door. The last thing I remember was looking over to see the boy fumbling with the lever of an old rifle.

Chapter 9

I was cold. Bone-chilling, aching, cold. I slowly awoke to realize I was lying under the edge of a pinion in a foot of snow. When I tried to move, my left arm and shoulder felt as if on fire. I laid back to ease the pain and realized this to be a mistake. It was the devil's own choice; freeze to death or tough out the pain. Well, I thought, it makes no difference. I'll not go far without my horse.

Then I realized my horse was standing, ground hitched, with the near side rein no more than a foot from my left hand. I tried to reach for the rein and again was stopped by the searing pain in my left side. I couldn't roll over to reach with my right hand, again stopped by the pain. I was finally able to turn myself as if on a center pivot like a crab. When I could reach my rein I found it not to be the braided leather made by my dad before he died, but, a plain piece of rope. I couldn't be bothered at that time. Slowly by inches I raised myself to where I could grab my stirrup. I felt the cold metal as I took hold and I wondered how that could be. My saddle was not new but it was a good one with full leather covering on the stirrup. Soon I was able to stand and when I was able to grope the saddle horn, I looked closer at my horse. My horse, but not my saddle or bridle. I couldn't be worried about those things. I had to get mounted and find help for my wound. Strangely when I stood and leaned to my left the pain subsided. Little at a time, I was able to get on my horse and as long as his gait was steady, I could ride without pain. I set my path by the North Star and soon the sky began to lighten.

Each time I felt myself losing consciousness, I'd raise my left shoulder slightly and the pain would bring me full awake. Thus it was, that in mid afternoon, I rode up to the Bailey cabin door. I sat there for a moment trying to work out the dryness in my mouth to call for help when the door opened and Miss Clatilda stepped out grabbing my horse bridle.

Strangely enough, getting off my horse was more difficult than mounting had been. Miss Clatilda helped me into the house and to bed. She stripped off my bloody shirt to reveal a wound that entered at the back side of my ribs and came out the meaty part below my left shoulder blade. As she cleaned the wound, it became apparent why certain movement caused so much pain. I had cracked ribs. When the wounds were bandaged, Miss Clatilda wrapped my torso tightly with a wide piece of cloth. I was then able to get almost total relief from the pain. The cold had probably saved my life for Miss Clatilda said the bullet's exit hole in my back was covered with frozen blood. Had it not been for this I would probably have bled to death.

Miss Clatilda took my horse into the barn to unsaddle. When she came into the house, it was with a question.

"Mr. Jackson, what happened to your good saddle and bridle?"

"What was on my horse?"

"An old granny saddle, dried almost as hard as wood, a thin used bedding blanket and a bridle pieced together by wire with cotton rope reins."

"Well, it would appear that our rustlers not only got away with cattle, they took my rig as well." I only wondered why they bothered.

I then told her the whole story, up to and including my ride home.

"Well, it doesn't matter. Day after tomorrow is Sunday, and I'll be seeing Bishop Terry. I'll ask him to send some of the men from the ward. We'll get my cattle, your saddle and bridle and all in due time."

"No, you won't!" I said, swinging my legs off the bed. "If you will lend me one of the saddles you keep in the barn, I'll have my rig, your cattle and that whole murderous bunch back here. Then we'll take them to town and they can do what they want with them."

"You're not well enough for such a ride, Will. If you reopen that wound on your back, you will bleed to death. You rest, I'll see this matter is resolved."

I said no more. I slipped into my coat and went to the barn where I got a clean shirt, saddled my horse and led him out to find Miss Clatilda coming out of the cabin.

"Ma'am, where did you put my rifle? I couldn't find it?"

"It was not on that old saddle. I suppose they must have stolen that also."

"May I borrow one of yours?" I said "I still have my pistol but I'd feel better with a rifle."

"Of course, but I thought you were not leaving until morning."

"I won't argue with you, Miss Clatilda. This is something I must do."

"I understand, Will. My only concern is for your well being. Please stable your horse and come in the house. I'll fix you a good supper then after a good night's sleep, you'll be better able to do what you must."

Two great meals, a good night's sleep and having my ribs re-wrapped found me in much better shape the next morning as I rode out.

I rode to within a good mile from the Taylor place. I could see smoke coming from their chimney and as I watched, I saw a figure come from the house and go into the barn. It came out moments later with what appeared to be a saddle. Sure enough the figure went into the coral and began saddling one of the horses.

I settled down behind a clump of pinion pines to see which way the rider went. I had not long to wait for he mounted and rode directly for me. When he got even with the pinions behind which I was hiding, I gigged my pony out in front of him and aimed my rifle right at Ray Taylor's belt buckle.

"Nice looking saddle you're riding, friend."

Taylor turned snow white and gulped a couple of times before he blurted out, "We was sure you'd be dead by now."

"Not so, friend, step down off that horse and stand easy."

It took but a few minutes for me to tie and gag Taylor. Then leading his horse, I rode into the door yard of his house. When I hailed the house, the door opened just enough for me to see the barrel of my Henry rifle being pushed out.

"Mister, I shot you once. You want me to do it again?"

"Wouldn't do that, Clendon. If you do, your Pa will freeze to death before you find him."

"You ain't got my Pa."

"Can't you see, boy? His horse is standing right here."

"What you done with my man, cowboy?" yelled Mrs. Taylor.

"Nothing, yet, ma'am. But, if you and that back-shooting boy of yours aren't standing outside here by the time I count to ten, you'll never see him alive again."

Both were on the ground in front of the steps before I could have counted to three.

"Now, where's my man?" demanded Blanche Taylor.

"I will take you to him as soon as Clendon saddles those two horses."

"Ain't got but one saddle mister," whined the boy.

"Fine, then you saddle the one for your mother, and you can ride bareback on the other."

"What about my baby, mister?" asked Blanche.

"Wrap her up good. It's going to be a cold ride."

"Mister, we got a buckboard. Will it be all right for me to hitch our horse up to it so my ma and little sister can ride in it?"

"That will be fine, but you'd better make it snappy. I expect your Pa is getting right cold."

While the boy harnessed the horse and hitched it to the buckboard, I changed my saddle from Taylor's horse to mine and put Miss Clatilda's saddle in the buckboard. I put the other worn out saddle on the horse Ray Taylor had been riding. I had the boy drive the buckboard. I didn't want any of them to ride Miss Clatilda's saddle.

I pushed the cattle on ahead and when the boy and his mother caught up I had Taylor on his horse with his hands tied to the saddle horn and his feet tied beneath the horse's belly.

"Mister, if that horse spooks, my daddy could get drug to death."

"Then, boy, you'd better drive carefully because I'm tying your daddy's horse to the back of your wagon."

Thus we rode into the Bailey's yard that evening after I had choused the four cows and the calf back into the herd as we rode by.

Miss Clatilda came out of the cabin, having heard the banging of the buckboard across the frozen ground.

"Mrs. Taylor, you take the baby on into the house. Clendon and I will take care of the horses."

I left Ray Taylor tied on his horse while the boy and I stabled the other horses. When we had hung the harnesses and put up Miss Clatilda's saddle, I surprised the boy by making him sit down beside a stall stanchion where I tied him tightly to that heavy timber. I then went out and got Taylor off his horse and brought him in and tied him to the stanchion directly across the barn alley from his son. I made the concession of lighting the stove in my room before leaving them, both complaining, while I went to the cabin to explain the situation to Miss Clatilda. I found her and Blanch Taylor, tending the Taylor baby.

I explained what had happened as Miss Clatilda prepared a bowl of stew and a glass of milk for me.

"Now, Miss Clatilda, I am going to have to ask you to watch Mrs. Taylor while I get a couple of hours of sleep. I'm afraid I can go no further right now. And, ma'am, watch her careful. I've no reason to trust her any more than her back-shooting boy."

I turned to Mrs. Taylor, "A word of advice. This lady is tougher than I am. You try anything with her and you may not live to settle your problems with the law. She owns the cattle you and your people stole. They were left to her by her late husband."

I stumbled out of the cabin, barely making it to my room in the barn before collapsing into a dead sleep on my bed.

I was shaken awake by Miss Clatilda in the full daylight of another day.

"Will, are you all right?"

I swung my feet off the edge of the bed and sat there while the cobwebs left my brain.

"Yes ma'am, I'm sorry to have conked out on you. Did you get any sleep last night?"

"Yes, as a matter of fact, I got a good night's sleep. I told Mrs. Taylor that all the stories she had heard about Mormons were true and that if she left, Brother Brigham's legions would hunt her and her family down and massacre them in their sleep. I don't believe Mrs. Taylor slept well. If you feel up to milking the cows and goat, I'll have breakfast ready when you're done."

As she turned to leave, I thought that this lady was the answer to a cowboy's dream. It was every cowboy's need to have a good horse. It was their dream to have a good horse that was also pretty. Miss Clatilda was not only strong but it appeared she had a good sense of humor, as strong a combination as a pretty, good horse.

Chapter 10

Tue to her word, Miss Clatilda had breakfast on the table when I brought the milk in.

"I have a plate for Mr. Taylor and his son. When you've eaten, I'm sure you would be the better one to untie them and watch them as they eat."

Mrs. Taylor offered to feed her man, but I told her that was one chore I would handle.

"Mr. Jackson, if you will hitch up my buggy, William and I will go into services while you take the Taylor's into the settlement." It was thus we pulled up in front of the meeting house, Bishop Terry, his brother and two other men came out from the crowd that was going into the building, and Miss Clatilda quietly explained the situation to Bishop Terry. Curiously, she did not mention my injury or the second trip I'd had to make to retrieve the cattle and the

Taylors.

"We'll have to arrange for the Taylors to stay with someone until we can figure out what to do with them," Bishop Terry said.

"No sir," I spoke up, "I don't think you want to do that. Where's the nearest sheriff?"

"Mr. Jackson, the nearest law officer is in Alamosa. That's a good hard two day ride from here. It would be best to put these people in with one of our families until we can get word to the sheriff and have him pick them up."

"Bishop, I'd be right concerned for the safety of any family with which you left this crew. I think they are not to be trusted, and I know for a fact they can be dangerous."

"Mr. Jackson, we have no facilities for the detention of this family. Also, I think I would balk at the idea of placing a woman and infant under lock and key."

I turned to the buckboard, "Mrs. Taylor, do you wish to stay here or will you go with your son and husband?"

"I ain't staying nowhere when my man and our boy are drug off somewhere else."

"Miss Clatilda, I'll be gone four or five days. Will that be all right?"

"Mr. Jackson, do you think it's absolutely necessary to take these people to a sheriff?"

"Ma'am, the one thing that cannot be tolerated by any rancher is rustling. These people have to be punished."

"Be careful, sir, and hurry back."

I knew the trip to Alamosa would be difficult, given the time of year and the weather, but I didn't expect the problems I had.

That first night, we made it to Del Norte, at the foot of Wolf Creek. We found an inn with two vacant rooms. I tied Ray and Clendon to the bed in one room and gave the other to Blanche and the baby. I slept on the floor, in front of the door in Ray and Clendon's room.

I was up before daybreak. I hoped to get to Alamosa before dark. When I knocked on Blanche's door, there was no answer. I knocked again, louder, but still no answer. I turned the knob and was surprised to see the door swing open. There was no one in the room and the bed appeared not to have been slept in.

I went into the front part of the bar and there found a group of people standing around Blanche Taylor, who was seated holding her baby.

"That's him!" she said, pointing at me.

Two of the men turned and started toward me. I noticed one had a star on his vest.

"Fellow, this here lady says you're taking her and her family to Alamosa on some wild goose chase to steal their homestead. What have you got to say about this?"

"I'm not stealing anything. These people stole cattle from my boss. What's more that woman's son back-shot me inside their own cabin. I was taking them to Alamosa to turn them over to the sheriff but as long as you're here, and if you're from any county around here, I'll just turn them over to you."

"Well, it's not going to be that easy, cowboy. That poor lady had to spend the night in a chair out here. She said you tied up her husband and son somewhere and told her to sit tight until morning."

"Friend," I asked, "did any of you think to talk to the innkeeper? He will tell you about the room I rented for Mrs. Taylor and her baby."

"Mrs. Taylor's already told us about that. She said you took that room for yourself."

"I'm going to ask one more time. Has anyone talked to the innkeeper?"

"Can't do that," spoke up a sallow faced youth from behind the counter, "He's gone to Pueblo to be with his sister. She's supposed to be dying."

I turned to the man wearing the star. "I'll tell you what, friend, I'll sign a formal complaint against this crew for rustling and also against the boy upstairs for back-shooting me. Then you do with them what you please."

"Where you from, cowboy?" asked the deputy.

"West of here, a good day's ride."

"You ain't one of them Mormons, that have that settlement over there, are you?"

"No, I'm not Mormon, but my boss is, and we live six or eight miles north of the settlement."

"I thought you Mormons were big on turning the other cheek. How come you want these folks punished?"

"I'll tell you why, friend, I'm not Mormon and I was cowboying years before I even knew what a Mormon was. Because of that, I know of only two ways to handle cow thieves; string them up, on the spot, or turn them over to the law. I wouldn't hang a man and his son and leave his wife and baby alone in that country. Now, you want me to make out a complaint and sign it or will you handle it?"

"How do you know these people stole cattle?"

"Because I found the cattle in their horse corral. Listen, friend, are you going to take these people into custody, or not?"

"Well now, cowboy, I'm going to have to check this whole matter out. I just can't go off half-cocked."

I turned to the crowd. "Is there a rancher here?"

One man spoke up, saying he had a "fair sized" spread down along the Conejos River.

"All right, sir, I'm going upstairs and untie Ray Taylor and his son, Clendon. From here on they are the responsibility of this lawman. If he chooses to let them go, I got a couple of suggestions for you; count your herd every day or so and don't let that back-shooting kid get behind you."

"Cowboy, you've said that a couple of times now. How do we know you're telling the truth?"

"That's easy friend," I said. "Look for yourself."

I lifted my jacket and shirt to expose the bandage covering my wounds.

"If you question my charge they stole cattle, ask this one here," I said pointing to Blanch Taylor, "about her theory about how to start a ranch with a long loop and a hot running iron."

"Well, cowboy," said the rancher, "those were Mormon cattle in Mormon country. Around here that does not make much difference."

Several of the bystanders raised their agreement with the rancher.

I turned and left the lobby returning to the room where Ray and Clendon were tied. I gathered my possessions, untied both and followed them to the lobby. When there, I singled out the lawman.

"Friend, I don't know what sort of peace officer you may be, but here are two rustlers. Keep them, release them, or whatever. But, this I'll tell them, and you. If I, or anyone I know has any problems with them returning to their 'homestead', if in fact, homestead it is, or, I find my boss' cattle in their corral ever again. Wife and baby or no, there's going to be a hanging."

A couple grumbled as I started to leave and the lawman even called for me to come back. But I just walked out, went to the stable and after I'd saddled my horse headed out of that place. It was only after I'd ridden a mile or so that I remembered I'd eaten nothing the night before and no breakfast.

"Well, partner," I thought, "next time, eat first, then start an argument with a roomful of people."

Chapter 11

A cold spell had settled in the night before and the ride back to the Bailey ranch was miserable. I arrived long after dark and thought to quietly go to bed and dream of Miss Clatilda's breakfast.

The cabin door opened as I rode up to the barn door.

"Is that you, Mr. Jackson?" she called.

"Yes ma'am, I'll see you in the morning."

"No, you won't. You'll come in here just as soon as you stable your horse." With that, she closed the cabin door.

I stabled my horse and I thought to go on to bed, but I knew she'd just come and chew me out. So, fifteen minutes after I arrived, I was standing at the cabin door.

"Come in here, sir, and tell me what happened," she said after opening the door.

I told her the whole story, while she fried me some eggs and an elk steak. When I'd told her the whole story, she asked if the lawman had taken them into custody. I told her I didn't rightly know but there was something troubling me.

"Miss Clatilda, before I came here, I never knew a Mormon. I'd heard stories, but they were so wild I didn't believe them anyway. But why were those people so dead set against you folks? You could tell it in every thing they said or did. You know, ma'am, I was relieved to be out of there without having to fight my way free of that mess."

"Mr. Jackson, I don't really know how to answer your question. People like those murdered our prophet, Joseph, and repeatedly ran our people out of their homes. There somehow, seems something about us that raises the hatred in some. I just don't know. When Jethro was alive, I discussed this with him. He said he thought it might have had somewhat to do with our comfort in what our Heavenly Father has given us."

"And, just what would that be, ma'am?"

"Well, Sir, we have a testament, other than the Bible, of the mission of Jesus."

"Other than the Bible? I've heard you folks don't believe in the Bible. Some say you have your own bible."

"Mr. Jackson, do you read much?"

"Yes, ma'am, but I don't own any books. So, I read just about anything else that comes along."

"I'm going to lend you a book to read. Please take care of it, as I have only the one copy. I can't tolerate it to be abused."

"I'd be careful with it, ma'am."

She rose from the table and went into her bedroom, returning with a book, somewhat smaller than most bibles I'd seen. She gave it to me, referring to it as "The Book of Mormon."

I finished my meal and, taking the book, went back to the barn and my room. I read some in the book that evening, but somehow reading the book made me uneasy.

When I got up the next morning, the first thing I noticed was how much warmer it was than it had been the night before. I half-expected what I found when I looked out the barn door. Six or eight inches of new snow and still coming down.

I milked the cows and the goat and when I stomped into the cabin, I found Miss Clatilda bathing the baby.

"Will, please go to the well and draw me a bucket of water, this is getting warm."

I turned to pick up a bucket when it hit me, "warm?" "You mean cold, don't you?"

"No, Will, William has a high fever, and I'm trying to bring it down with a cold sponge bath."

I was a little put off by that treatment but I went out after the cold well water. And let me tell you, well water, in that high country, that time of year was cold indeed.

When I returned to the kitchen, Miss Clatilda had me empty the pan and fill it with the cold water. She held the boy and gently washed him with a rag frequently dipped in the dishpan of icy water.

I took the time to restock the wood box and build up the fire, warming up the cabin.

"Ma'am," I asked, "have you been up long with the boy?"

"I'm afraid so. I noticed his fever right after you went to bed. I've been working all night to bring it down."

"Is he coughing or anything?"

"No, and that's what's strange. He doesn't seem to have anything wrong except this fever."

I reached over and touched the baby's forehead, then placed the back of my hand against my head.

"Ma'am, this baby has no fever. He's cool to the touch."

She placed the baby in the center of the table and went to the stove where she warmed her hand, red with the cold from the water.

When she returned to the table she felt of the boy's head, then lifting his gown felt of his body. The relief on her face was so obvious. She then went to the cupboard and made a bottle of the fresh goat's milk and fed young William. He seemed to have no trouble eating. When she put him back in his basket, she returned to the kitchen.

"Now, Mr. Jackson, I expect you're hungry."

"Yes ma'am, and if you'll allow it, I'll fry us some eggs and elk. It won't be as good as when you cook, but it'll let you rest and we'll get by."

"Oh, no, Mr. Jackson, I'd be ashamed to have you prepare a meal for yourself and for me."

"Well, be ashamed, but do it quietly. I'm not very good at this, and I've got to concentrate."

As I was dishing up the eggs I looked over and she had her head on the table and was obviously sound asleep. I hated to awaken her, but I felt she needed to eat in order to keep up her strength. While we were eating, I noticed how very tired she was.

"Miss Clatilda, it's snowing hard now so there is little I can do outside. Why don't I bring some of my small work in here? That way you can get some much needed sleep, and I'll watch out for William. If there's any change or a problem, I'll awaken you."

"Will, I should not do this but I am going to accept your offer. Just stack the dishes, I'll wash them when I get up."

She went to her bedroom immediately after breakfast. I brought my work in from the barn and, all in all, the three of us had a restful morning. William awakened midmorning and I brought his basket in closer to the kitchen stove, and he went right back to sleep.

At noon I had a sandwich made from the meat left from breakfast and after working a while longer was wondering if I shouldn't get something for William. I was also wondering if I would know how to feed "the infant."

I heard a noise and Miss Clatilda was standing in the doorway

"Mr. Jackson, have you ever considered taking a wife?"

I wanted to run so bad my knees ached. I didn't know what else to do.

Finally, I got the courage to answer, "No ma'am, I'm afraid not. I have nothing, not even prospects, to offer a woman."

"Well, I was just thinking, you would make a good husband. Few are sufficiently compassionate to do what you did this morning and fewer still are conscientious enough to do their work at the same time."

"Thank you, ma'am, but if you're all right now, I'll ride down and have a look at the cattle. I believe it has stopped snowing."

"Will you be having a bite to eat before you go?"

"No, ma'am, I had a sandwich earlier."

I got out of that cabin as soon as I could grab up the harnesses and bridles I'd been working on. In fifteen minutes I was riding south toward where the cattle were pastured.

This time, I counted the herd immediately, and twice. They were all there. I rode among them for an hour or so and, with the exception of having to lance the cheek of one of the calves where it had gotten a fox tail hung in behind its molars, the herd seemed in good shape.

I returned to the barn, where much cleaning was needed. It was almost dark by the time I had laid new straw in the stanchions. Miss Clatilda stuck her head in the barn door to tell me to come to supper.

Chapter 12

It was interesting that Miss Clatilda offered grace over every meal, but most interesting was that about half the time she asked me to say the prayer. At first I was awkward and uncomfortable but as time went on, I became more and more comfortable with the observance. No less awkward, but more comfortable.

As winter turned into spring my work load continued to increase. I welcomed the Sundays when Miss Clatilda and William were gone most of the day to church meetings in the settlement. I would begin my work before the buggy was out of sight and be tapering off by mid-afternoon so I could stop immediately when I heard or saw the buggy returning. Miss Clatilda was still not pleased with my working on Sunday.

Every Sunday, after supper, I'd go to my room and read a couple of hours in the book Miss Clatilda loaned me. Most, in that book, made good reading. I could not, however, get over the feeling that something was not right.

By mid-April most of the herd had calved out and the new calf crop was doing great. We only lost two calves. One stillborn and the other was born during a howling thunderstorm. Little guy didn't have a chance.

I was talking to Miss Clatilda one morning at breakfast about the calf crop, "ma'am, I could sure use some help when it comes time to work the calves. They have to be branded and all."

"How many men will you need, Will?"

"Ma'am, that depends on what you can afford. Two or three would be nice but we can make do with one."

"How would six or seven suit you, Mr. Jackson?"

"Right down to the ground! But it would also eat up a lot of the profit on what calves you sell."

"Oh, there'll be no cost for the men, Mr. Jackson. They will only cost us their breakfast and dinner."

"Ma'am, we'll need people who have worked cattle; not a bunch of kids."

"That's true. But we have almost sixty families in our ward. Over two thirds have farms or ranches. All I must do is give them ten days or two weeks notice, and you will have as many men as you need. I know this will happen for it has been so, for each of the four years I've lived on this ranch."

"I'll be darned. You mean Bishop Terry wasn't just making 'burying talk?' You mean you could actually get a half dozen men, not boys, to help with the branding?"

"Yes, sir, and all I'll need is two weeks notice so the men can have time to schedule their work to free up as many days as you will need them."

That afternoon I went up behind the cabin and dropped about thirty lodge pole pine. When I got back to the barn with my load of trees, Miss Clatilda came out to see what I was doing.

"Well, Miss Clatilda, I thought if all those men were coming, they might want to bring their families. If you and the ladies should want to sit outside, I thought I'd put up a brush arbor so you'll be out of the sun. It won't take long. I should have it all done except for laying the brush on top by noon tomorrow. I hope that will be all right, ma'am."

"Mr. Jackson, let's you and I get one thing straight. I need your promise to do something for me, if you will."

"Ma'am, I'll try."

"Will Jackson, from this moment on I want you not ever to call me Miss Clatilda, Mrs. Bailey or anything other than my given name: Clatilda. Just that, Will, and I will do likewise. I have swayed between 'Will' and 'Mr. Jackson' enough. Our friendship and mutual respect would seem to require at least this one small concession to propriety."

I didn't rightly know what to say, and I sure didn't know what 'propriety' meant.

"Ma'am, that's fine with me, but what might Bishop Terry say to such familiarity?"

"He would probably say, while he was holding a calf for you to brand, that it would make a lot of sense for you to say, 'Alton, hold that calf still; than for you to address him as Bishop Terry."

"Clatilda, it may take me a while but I'd be pleased and honored to call you by your given name. Also, ma'am, will it be all right to go ahead with the brush arbor?"

"I also don't care for 'ma'am', Will. I am neither your mother or your old maid school teacher."

"Well, then, I'm sorry. I'll probably call you 'ma'am' to the last day I know you. That I couldn't give up, when talking to a lady, to save my life."

"All right, Will, but no more 'Miss Clatilda,' please. And yes, please do build a brush arbor. I think it will be a grand thing. Also, when you brand, will you please dress out a steer that we might have fresh meat for the meals we will serve?"

"Nope."

"What do you mean, Mr., er, Will?"

"You sure wanted to say 'Mr. Jackson' didn't you?"

She just smiled and nodded her head. I told her of the herd of elk I'd been watching in the timber, southeast of her place and that I intended to knock down a bull or two to provide fresh roasted elk for the day it would take to work the calves.

Chapter 13

It took a little longer than I'd planned to erect the arbor framework. I finished up just before supper time the next day.

Mid-afternoon, while I was stringing the cross posts on top of the arbor, Bishop Terry's nephew rode up to the cabin and talked to Clatilda for a few minutes, then left. I paid no attention as I figured if he had business with me he'd come to where I was. He didn't.

At supper that evening, Clatilda said we had some planning to do. Bishop Terry had sent word for all the farmers and ranchers to come prepared to discuss what schedules they had for haying season. That would be so that every man might be able to plan his work and when he would be able to help others.

"Ma'am, right off the top of my head I haven't any idea when we will be ready to hay. There are five fields and all are doing well for the time of year, but when to cut will depend on a lot of things."

"Would it help if you knew when Mr. Bailey did it for the past four years?"

"That'd make all the difference in the world. Then we would, at least, have something to start with."

"Good! Then I'll go through Jethro's journal this evening. I'll have those dates for you in the morning."

"What's a journal, ma'am?"

"It's like a diary, Will. I keep one and so did Jethro. You simply write down what you do or experience or even what you think, every day. That is, those things that seem, or are, important to you."

"That seems a handy thing to do. Make a fellow feel good ten or twelve years from now to be able to know what he did on this day."

"That's the idea, Will. We need to know who we are and where we're going."

"Yeah, and it'd be nice to know where we came from, too."

"We already know that, Will."

I let that pass but, later, I thought about it some.

"Clatilda, how would a fellow get hold of a blank journal?"

"It so happens, I have a brand new bound book with four hundred blank pages. You may have it."

"I'd really like it but those things probably don't come cheap. Would you please take the cost out of my wages?"

"I can do that, Will, but I'd much rather make you a gift of the book."

"Whatever you think is fair, ma'am. But, as I said, I'd really like to have it. This journal seems such a good idea. I've always carried a tally book, but that's a working book. To have a book in which you could write for pleasure, now that's such a seemly thing."

Clatilda got right up from the table and went into her bedroom. She returned with a dark gray book about ten by fourteen inches.

She also had a quill pen and a small bottle of ink. She sat at the table and opened the book. Inside on the first page she wrote something then blotted the ink with her apron and gave me the book, quill and ink.

"Now, Will, you have all you need to begin your 'pleasure writing'."

"Well, what with my reading and now my 'journal' I'd best be getting to my room."

"Are you still reading the Book of Mormon?"

"Yes ma'am, but I've got to admit there is something about it that bothers me."

"Don't you like the stories?"

"Oh yes, I get real involved sometimes and sometimes I feel real funny. Not upset or put out or anything like that. It's hard to explain, but sometimes I'll read two or three pages then I'll just have to stop. I don't know why, I just have to think about what I've read."

"Should you come upon anything you'd like to discuss, we'll make time to talk about it."

"I appreciate that, ma'am. But, I'm afraid I'm going to have to wait until I can put a label on what's bothering me."

"That's fine, Will. The offer is there, if, you ever need someone to talk to."

I went to my room and there I opened the book to find what she had written. In very small and precise hand was written, "Given to Will Jackson on this the fourteenth day of May 1878 so his pleasure may be shared, with joy, by his posterity, Clatilda Bailey."

"Well, now," I thought, "that's just fine."

Chapter 14

At the table the next morning, Clatilda had all the haying dates
for the last four seasons. When we compared them, we found each
year's dates compared remarkably with all other years. We discussed
this some and in answer to my questions she said this past winter had
been a little bit lighter than in the past but not too bad. She said the
mountains seemed to have enough snow for a good run-off to keep
the streams full well into summer. Therefore, irrigating should not be
too difficult.

"You mean you irrigate those hay fields?"

"Oh surely, Will, Jethro took rather unseemly pride in the canals
he'd dug."

"I haven't seen any canals, and I've been all over this ranch."

"That's another thing Jethro was proud of. He said he didn't want
to have to drive his wagon all 'round robin hood's barn', as he put it,

just to get from one spot to another on his own place. If you will look for them, you will find the canals. They seem more low spots than ditches, but I assure you, they work quite well."

That explained the similar dates for haying. With just a little sunshine, and water when you needed it a fellow could probably schedule his haying efforts four or five years in advance. I told Clatilda so.

We settled on three dates using the periods Jethro Bailey had set aside in previous years. Clatilda wrote this on a sheet of paper then turned to me, "Will, I'm going to have to ask a big favor of you. I hope you'll understand and not mind too much."

"Yes, ma'am?"

"Will, I need you to go to church with me this Sunday."

"Oh, that's no problem, I'll be happy to drive you and William to your meetings."

"No, Will, I mean I want you to attend our meetings. At least, one in particular."

"Will I have to become a Mormon?"

She laughed that seldom heard, lilting chuckle of hers.

"No, Will, you won't have to become a Mormon. But, there is one meeting, not open to the women, at which the haying schedules will be discussed. That's actually the meeting I need you to attend. I could give the dates to the Bishop, but I'd prefer it if you took them."

"Ma'am, it will be a new experience for me. I've not been in a meetinghouse in almost twenty years. But if that's what you want, I'll do it."

I had no fancy clothes but, in the best I had, we left the ranch that

Sunday morning with everything in that buggy shining including the horse, buggy wheels, harness and me.

As we drove to town Clatilda told me the meeting she wanted me to attend would be held in a room adjacent to Bishop Terry's office, and I should seek out Bishop Terry or his brother and explain my presence.

This seemed very awkward to me, but John Terry put me immediately at ease and introduced me as Mrs. Bailey's ranch foreman to the forty-five or fifty men in the meeting. Not individually but as a group. He said it wouldn't take long for me to get to know the 'brethren'.

I couldn't believe the organization of that group. They had two large blackboards upon which had been drawn the four months; June, July, August, and September with a good sized block for each day of each month. We all were assigned numbers, all who would have need of help for haying. These numbers were written in the daily blocks we referenced. Bishop Terry asked if anyone present had requirements for help they had not needed the previous year. When no one responded he said good, that meant we would be dealing with the same number of men.

When he had everything posted, then there came a surprisingly short period of juggling dates and manpower. In less than half an hour I had a list in my hand of men to help in the three cuttings I hoped to get and that Bailey had gotten in the past. I was to be given ten men each of the planned days. Additionally, I was assigned fourteen days in the hayfields of other folks.

When the meeting was over Bishop Terry prayed for, what seemed to me, an awful long time. But when he was through, every man in that room said 'amen', so I guess I just wasn't used to that kind of praying.

Chapter 15

John Terry stopped me after the meeting in which we had settled the haying schedule.

"You know you and Sister Bailey are to have dinner at my home, don't you?"

"No, sir, I figured just to hang around until Mrs. Bailey was ready to leave for home."

"That's not to be done. You come on with me, I'm sure Sister Bailey has gone on home with my wife."

It was a short walk to John's home, hard beside the general store. We went in and found Mrs. Terry and Clatilda working in the kitchen.

Before dinner, John and I went into his parlor and sat, enjoying the quiet afternoon.

"John, what do the rest of the people who live out of town do in this period between your meetings?"

"Some live close enough to go home, some picnic on the church meeting grounds, weather permitting. Oh, there are a variety of activities to keep them busy. Usually, in addition to Sister Bailey, we will have five or six for dinner and visiting afterward."

We lapsed into an uneasy silence for fifteen or twenty minutes until there came a knock on Terry's front door. John escorted a group of seven adults and at least that many children into the parlor. John introduced them all to me. The women and girls headed immediately to the kitchen where, soon, there was much chattering.

I sat quietly by while the men discussed cattle and farming. Finally, Emil Glaston turned to me and asked if I was the one working Jethro Bailey's ranch.

"Yes, Mrs. Bailey hired me right after Mr. Bailey was killed."

"Understand you killed the bear that did, for Jethro," said Glaston.

"Yes, but not soon enough."

"Can't be helped! At least you were there to help the ladies through the worst part of the ordeal."

"Sir, in my opinion, neither one needed much help. They both were exceptionally strong."

"Well, we know where that strength comes from, don't we, Brother Terry? Has anyone talked to you about our gospel, Mr. Jackson?"

"That's being taken care of, Brother Glaston." Clatilda said from the dining room, where she was setting the table.

"Well, now, Sister Bailey, it could be we could help this good man in ways other than what you might," said Glaston.

"That will be fine, Brother Glaston, and should we find need of help in those areas, I will be the first to contact you."

Clatilda stood, plates in one hand and the other full of silverware. She seemed to be awaiting additional comment from Glaston. But, he turned to Terry and began discussing fencing wire. Somehow I felt myself a pawn.

Dinner had seemed strained and after dinner most sat in the Terry parlor quietly reading or talking. It dawned on me, finally, after the women had cleaned the kitchen, after dinner, that there was inequality between the number of men and women. Including Terry, his son and myself there were eight women and five men. I could find no explanation for this other than one or more of the men had more than one wife. That really made me uncomfortable.

After the men's meeting, and as we headed back to the ranch, I asked Clatilda about the number of women at Terry's.

"Two of them are Brother Terry's wives. The tall black haired woman is one and the other you met. Three of the others are Emil Glaston's wives. The other two are John Berdon's. He was the other man at the Terry's."

I sat quietly thinking about this for the rest of the way back to the ranch.

"Will, I have a dried apple pie I made last evening before I retired. Would you like a piece with a little cream on top?"

"Always! I'll be in as soon as I put the buggy and horse away."

When I went in, she had a big piece of pie with an abundance of cream on top and, wonder of wonders, a steaming hot cup of coffee.

I sat down and as much as I enjoyed the pie, I really enjoyed the coffee.

"Ma'am, how did you come by coffee in this area? I would have thought it to be unavailable."

"Brother Terry stocks a little for non LDS people who live east of here. I felt it to be only fair that I prepare it for you, although for me to join you would be to break a commandment of the Lord."

"Ma'am, I had to memorize the ten commandments when I was a kid. I don't remember anything about; 'Thou shalt not drink coffee'!"

"You would not have known of this commandment, Will. As a matter of fact it has not always been a commandment. Not to drink coffee and tea was part of a revelation given to our first prophet, Joseph Smith."

"Is he the 'Brother Joseph,' I hear people talking about?"

"Yes, Will, he founded our church as a result of other revelations he received from the Lord. The revelation about coffee and tea also contains other restrictions on what we eat and other products we should not use or use only in moderation. Originally it was given to Brother Joseph as a suggestion that even the weakest of the saints should be able to follow. It was then given as a revelation to another of our prophets, Brigham Young, that the original revelation be strengthened. So, at a general conference of our members Brother Brigham presented it as a commandment of the Lord, and it has been treated as such by the Saints ever since."

"Clatilda, I remember reading of prophets of Bible times, but I thought the time for them had passed."

"So do a lot of other people, Will. Our belief in modern day prophecy has caused my people almost continuous harassment. We believe that the president of our church is a modern day prophet of God and His mouthpiece here on earth."

"You know, that's almost as good as the journal. Must be a sight of comfort to your people to have him."

"Oh, yes it is Will, even though it is hard sometimes to follow his directions."

"Ma'am, I've been wanting to ask you something ever since we left the Terry's. What was that all about, between you and Glaston, before we had dinner?"

"That was a cow with two sets of horns, Will. You sure you want to hear the whole story?"

"Well, yes ma'am, if it doesn't cause you any problems."

"It won't cause me problems, but you may have some trouble putting it all in perspective."

I had no idea what "perspective" meant, but I sensed more was to be said than had been said.

"You go ahead, ma'am, should it be I get in over my head, I'll yell for help."

Clatilda smiled that sweet smile of hers and stepping to the stove refilled my cup.

"Will, first off, I'll explain my animosity toward Emil Glaston."

"Ma'am, as you know, I'm just a cowboy, there's lots of words I can say and even read, but that don't mean I understand. What does 'animosity' mean?"

"I'm sorry, Will. I spent several years preparing myself to be a school teacher. I forget myself. I hope you know I do not mean to offend you."

"No, ma'am, I'm not upset, it's just that some big words throw me."

"All right, Will. Did you notice that Emil Glaston and I are not the best of friends?"

"Yes, ma'am, that came through right clear."

"The reason for the undercurrent of dislike is that over Christmas when I had little William in the settlement, Emil Glaston came to me at John Terry's and proposed that I become his fourth wife."

"What was he after, your ranch?"

Clatilda glanced sharply at me with a strange look on her face.

"You know, Will, I was so upset by a man with three wives already, trying to make me his fourth, I hadn't thought of that possibility. There are some things I know about Brother Glaston that make your observation quite plausible . . . that is, it makes what you say, possibly, true."

"I was just thinking, Glaston has neither the youth nor the good looks to tempt someone like you. It would seem that your 'dowry' might persuade an older man to look on you with much favor."

"Will, I had not thought to have this conversation until some later time. It appears now is that time. Have you ever heard the expression 'celestial marriage'?"

"Marriage yes, 'celestial marriage,' no."

"It is a program, established by the founder of our church, Joseph Smith."

"I thought this 'Brother Brigham you're always talking about is the head of your church?"

"No, Will, even Brother Brigham has passed on. He was the president of our church after Brother Joseph was assassinated in Missouri."

"This 'celestial marriage' program was established so that every woman might have a provider and husband in this life and in what you probably know as 'Heaven'."

I sat for a minute and thought on that one.

"Ma'am, I can see a lot of trouble in that right off. I'd suspect the government might just act as if their belt was cinched up too tight, were they to come to know about it."

"Oh, they have, Will, and as you say they, and their leaders in Washington City, back east, have put many a good man in prison over this very thing."

"Clatilda, what do you think of this practice?"

"You forget, Will, I was married to a man who had two wives."

"Ma'am, I didn't aim to upset you. It's just that I forgot, and you being so independent, and all."

"That's all right. Mine was a perfect example of why this program was established. I arrived in Salt Lake City, having joined the Church in Kentucky, almost broke, sick with a fever and knowing no one except those I had met on the way out to Salt Lake City. My bishop took me and another single lady into his home. It was there I met Jethro Bailey who had been directed to come and settle this country along with twelve other families. I prayed about the suggestion Bishop Hamill had made. While there were many sides of the problem I did not care for there were sufficient grounds to declare the situation to be the best for my circumstances."

"You mean, Mr. Bailey was already married to Miss Jennifer?"

"Yes, they had been married over a year."

"But she didn't look a day over sixteen or seventeen!"

"It was amazing how young she looked, wasn't it. Jennifer and I were the same age when she died."

"My mother used to say that no kitchen was big enough to hold two women. How did you two get along?"

"There was work enough for two. It helped to keep busy."

"Pardon me for saying so, ma'am, but that would seem to me to be an almost unworkable situation."

"It is, Will, if you have not the Church to support you. This is particularly true of those good sisters whose husbands are in prison."

"Would you ever marry a man with wife or wives again?"

"If things stay the same or get better than they are now, the answer to that is no. That is, unless I was directed to do so by an authority of my church."

"You mean like Bishop Terry?"

"Yes, but that is not very likely, what with the government hounding all known polygamists."

I pushed back from the table to leave, but she stopped me.

"Will, there are a few other things I would discuss with you, if you're not too tired."

"No ma'am. The hardest thing I've done all day was hitch and unhitch the team."

"Do you remember when Brother Glaston asked if anyone had

spoken to you about the gospel?"

"Yes'm, but I don't know what he meant."

"How are you coming along with the book I loaned you?"

"Fine, ma'am, I'm about three quarters through. But, in all honesty, there is still something that bothers me when I read it."

"Bothers you, how?"

"Ma'am, I can't rightly put my finger on it. Just something's missing or something I don't understand."

"You continue to read, Will, and if you want to talk, I'm here. Now, about the gospel. As you may know, Will, every church has rules and guidelines by which they worship. Ours is no different. Our rules and guidelines are contained in our gospel. We believe that everything we are, or do, must be in obedience to our Heavenly Father's hopes and desires as brought to us by Jesus. Do you understand what I'm saying, Will?"

"I believe you're saying you try to run your church and your lives according to the Bible."

"Not just the Bible, Will, also the book you are reading."

"Well, we'll see, ma'am. I'm trying to finish the book by the end of haying season. Then we'll talk more."

Chapter 16

I spent a troubled night, but the next morning gave me something else to worry about.

When I went to take the milk into the house, I noticed smoke over in the southwest end of the valley. I pointed it out to Clatilda when she opened the door.

"Is it a forest fire?" she asked.

"No, the smoke is in a column and too small for a forest fire. Maybe you'd better just hold my breakfast for a while. I'll saddle up and go take a look."

"Be careful, Will."

As I rode down the valley, I saw yet another column of smoke, south of the first one.

I rode to the northern-most smoke first. When I reached it, I rode into a make-shift camp. There was a man, woman and at least three or four kids.

"Mr.," I said as the man stepped toward me, "what are you doing on this land?"

"Why, cowboy, we're homesteading. I've found this little sweet water stream on the good flat land east of here and we're here to put down roots."

"Do you know you're on private property?"

"Mr. Johnson over to Alamosa said you ranchers would probably try to run us off. But, cowboy, we ain't going. We got the United States government behind us. Why, by now, Mr. Johnson will already have filed our homestead papers. You're just too late, cowboy."

I said not another word but turned my pony and rode out toward the southern column of smoke. It was the same story there.

I rode back into the door yard and before I could step off my horse Clatilda was at the door.

"What is it, Will?"

"We may have real trouble, ma'am. Let's step inside and I'll explain it."

When we were inside, and Clatilda was fixing my breakfast, I explained what I had found and what the two settlers had told me.

"Ma'am, do you have deed to this property?"

"Yes, I do, and the deed is even registered in Alamosa. I also had the quit claim deed Jethro had signed for Jennifer and me; both filed by Bishop Terry when he went to Alamosa last January. I have deed to a little over twenty-eight hundred acres."

"Then your place, must be long and skinny because it has to be four or five miles to those haystacks south of here."

"Yes, its width extends only about a hundred feet into the tree line on both sides of the valley."

"Ma'am, if you don't mind me asking, why do you have so much land for your herd?"

"Jethro bought the land to close this valley to any others than the members of our church. Jethro's father had died, back east, leaving him an estate nearly sufficient to buy this land, stock it and put up the buildings. We have agreed with Bishop Terry to sell up to one thousand acres to whomever from our church wishes to buy."

"Pardon my asking, ma'am, but what does Bishop Terry have to do with it?"

"Will, you remember I told you there were twelve families originally came into this area?"

"Yes, that was when you and Mr. Bailey got married."

"Right. Well those twelve families bought the whole large valley into which this small valley, and it's creeks, feed. We bought in such a way that would keep others from causing the saints the problems they had back East."

"Who are the 'saints', ma'am?"

"We call our church, The Church of Jesus Christ of Latter-day Saints. Thus, we refer to each other as 'saints'."

"Taking a bit much on yourselves, aren't you?"

"No, I don't think so, Will. What we call each other may possibly be more what we want to be than what we are."

"Do you have a copy of that deed?"

"Yes, I do. The original is in John Terry's safe at his General Store. But Jethro had a certified copy made to keep here on the ranch."

"Are there property markers?"

"Yes, Jethro and Bishop Terry set rock and brass rod markers at each of the four corners of the ranch, after the surveyor had set his marks."

"Oh, the ranch is square?"

"No, Will, it is rectangular. It's longer north to south than east to west."

"Ma'am, do you own a compass?"

"Yes, Jethro had a very good marine compass, and I know right where it is."

"Then, if you will let me borrow it and point me toward one of those markers, I'll see if those settlers are on your property."

"I'll do better than that, William and I are both in need of an outing. We'll go with you and show you both the northwest and the northeast markers so your job will be easier and quicker."

We went in an open buggy as it was such a pleasant day. William was very excited to see everything and could hardly sit still, but with Clatilda directing the way, the two corners were found and quite easily, in spite of Williams' humorous distractions. I was relieved to see that the corners were plainly marked with stone mounds and metal rods. We returned to the house in good spirits just in time for lunch, after which Clatilda gave me the copy of her deed to examine.

"Now, ma'am, the legal description of your ground is easy

enough to follow. I'm no surveyor but I can read a property description, and I can read a compass. I am almost certain that both of those camps are on your property. What would you have me do?"

"I will not tolerate anyone stealing what my family worked so hard to build. But, on the other hand, I want to stay within the law. If they won't move peaceably, maybe we should go to Alamosa and see what the courts will do."

"Ma'am, you're wrong. By the time the law gets around to doing anything to help you Mormons in this country, both of those farmers will have made at least three crops. That's in addition to losing twenty-five or thirty of your cows, which they will have stolen and sold or eaten."

"All right, Will, what would you do?"

"Plain and simple. I'd go down there this afternoon and see that they're gone, lock, stock and barrel before nightfall."

"And if they refused to leave?"

"I'm fairly certain I can put it to them in such a way they will leave."

"I would be very upset if there were bloodshed, Will."

"Ma'am, let's you and I, finally, have an understanding. You hired me to run this ranch. To me that also means protecting it from any kind of thief. That means people like the Taylors, who stole your cows and people like those two sets of squatters, who are trying to steal your land. You can go to court if you want to. When, and if, you get there, you're going to have to prove your side, and then prove what these two outfits are doing. That means you have to deal with both sides of the question. If I kick them off, then they have the same two sides to deal with. But then it's their problem."

"That's quite a speech, Will. I think I've not heard you say so much, ever."

I looked at her and that mischievous smile, and I knew I'd never know such a woman again.

"Well, ma'am, what will it be?"

"All right, Will. First, you take the compass and make absolutely sure they are on our land. If you find they are, please see that they leave. I would hope this matter can be done without bloodshed. But, as you said, Will, I did hire you to run this ranch. So, as soon as you are ready, you'd best be about your job."

I sat for a moment and was, more than ever, impressed by the strength of this woman.

I rode to the northwest marker and then, according to the deed, lined up on true south-southeast on the compass, and started riding to the southwestern marker twenty-three thousand feet away. I wasn't quite sure how to measure that distance but I realized I didn't have to. If I ran into either settler before I got to that southwest marker, they would, in fact, be on the J-B Ranch.

Chapter 17

I rode over a small knoll and found myself a good three, maybe three hundred and fifty yards west of the northern settlers' camp. Rather than do anything at that time, I chose to continue on the compass setting, I rode on south. About a mile further I came upon the second camp. This one was at least fifteen hundred feet into the J-B. Just to be sure I rode on to the southwest marker. I hit it, dead on. The cairn of rocks, centered by the bronze rod was visible three or four hundred feet before I arrived at it. I rode my horse right up to where his nose was exactly over the rod. And then I pointed my pony north.

I figured to deal with the north camp first. I did not want anyone between me and Clatilda, if there was trouble. I rode into their camp out of the forest on their west side.

When I rode into that camp, I found the man and two boys about ten and twelve laying rocks for the foundation of a building.

"Getting ready to build, are you?" I said by way of greeting.

"Yeah cowboy, its part of the proving-up we have to do to make our homestead legal."

"Mister, you're never going to have a 'legal' homestead where you are now."

"Oh yes I am, cowboy. Mr. Johnson said you Mormons would try to give us trouble, but he said all we had to do was get in touch with him and he'd bring a federal marshal down on you like a swarm of bees."

"Well mister, you better be looking for a hollow log, 'cause you've got one hour to get off this ranch. Now, I ain't no lawyer, so I'm not going to discuss the issue. I will wait right here while you pack up and git!"

Then's when I heard the rifle being cocked. Without a second thought, or even a breath, I drew and cocked my six-gun and pointed it right at that man's middle.

"I don't know who's standing behind me with a cocked weapon but I'll give you about three heart beats to be standing in front of me with that weapon on the ground."

"Or what, cowboy," came a woman's voice from behind me.

"Or, I'll gut-shoot this man. If he's yours, you'd best think it over."

"Do what he says, Fannie. It ain't worth the gamble," the man said.

The woman stepped around me and reluctantly laid a rifle on the ground in front of where she then stood.

I looked around at the camp. The only items that had been

unloaded from the big Conestoga were a few tools and a cast iron stove.

"All right, now, you have thirty minutes to be on the move. I'll not tell you again and what's not gone from here in one-half hour, I'll burn or destroy. That's the end of my talking. Also, anyone lay a hand on that rifle or any other weapon I'll shoot first and discuss the burying later."

During that half hour I learned two things; the man's name was Rob Wilson and that Rob and Fannie Wilson were whiners.

When they had loaded their wagon, they started to head north. I swung along side and told Wilson he would go south.

"We can go this way and across a little pass," he said. "That's the way we came in."

"That's not the way you are going out. Now turn that wagon around before I really lose my temper."

I watched the Wilsons until they were well down the road toward the settlement. Then I turned and rode toward the second camp.

When I rode into the camp, all were gathered around a make-shift bed of pine-boughs. A small child was under the covers and was being ministered to by an older woman.

"What can we do for you, now?" a man said, stepping away from the bed.

"You got sickness in your camp?"

"Yeah, our little boy broke his leg playing on the rocks by the stream. We set it, but he's still in a lot of pain. It only happened an hour, or so, ago."

"Mister, I'm right sorry to hear that. Particularly because I bring you more bad news."

"What's wrong?"

"You're trespassing on private property, and you're going to have to move on."

"I am on this land fair and square. I signed homestead papers, and Tim Johnson, over to Alamosa, filed them almost three weeks ago. He told us you Mormons would try to run us out of this valley. Well friend, I don't run. You want me out of here, you're going to have to chase me, and, for a long time now, I haven't chased right easy."

"Mister, I don't know this Johnson fellow who's trying to run a sandy on every one, but I do know where the boundary markers are for the ranch whose deed is filed in the Alamosa Court House, and partner, you're near a quarter of a mile inside those boundary markers."

"If we pulled back west a quarter mile would that satisfy you?"

"Mister, once you're off this ranch, it's none of my business."

"Just where would you say your ranch's west line lies?"

"Well, I rode the line not three hours ago. My horse's tracks should be clear. Let's you and me ride over, and I'll show you."

The man took a bridle from the wagon and swung upon one of his draft horses, and we splashed across the creek and up into the trees. When we came to my horses tracks, He stopped and dismounted.

"This won't do. It won't do at all," he said.

"Maybe you just located wrong. Maybe this was where Johnson intended you to homestead."

"How can I farm this? It's all up and down and covered with trees and rocks. Why there ain't even water. Mr. Johnson already said our homestead should straddle the creek that runs in the west side of this valley."

"Well mister, I'm sorry as I can be about what this Johnson fellow told you, but that creek is smack dab inside the J-B Ranch."

"Well, that's just too bad. I've got a homestead there. If you don't like it, then talk to Tim Johnson and the judge in Alamosa."

"Friend," I said turning my horse to face him, "I'm going to tell you something. I'm only going to say it once, so pay close attention. You are trespassing on J-B land. You have until sundown, tomorrow to be gone. I'd give you the half hour I gave the Wilsons were it not for your little boy. I'll be back late tomorrow. If I find you here, I'll run you off just like I would any other thief."

"You ain't calling me no thief, and you ain't running me anywhere. I'll have the law on you so fast, you won't know what hit you."

"The closest law is in Alamosa. You do what you will, but I'm not warning you again. Tomorrow afternoon had better not find you here."

Chapter 18

Iturned my pony and rode back toward home. When I rode into the door yard, Clatilda stepped out, shielding her eyes with her hand as she watched me.

"What happened, Will?"

I explained the whole situation to her. She was concerned mostly about the child with a broken leg.

"Will, do you think, maybe, there is something I could do if I went down there?"

"I don't know, ma'am, but it is not something I would suggest you do. I left the man with a deadline of tomorrow, sundown, to be off your property. He may not go willingly."

"Will, I feel very badly about forcing someone with an injured child to load up a wagon and travel. Who knows how far, before they can settle again."

"I know, but I've told him to be gone tomorrow. If we back down, I don't think things will get better, only worse."

"Hitch up the buckboard, Will. I'll gather a few things. We're going down there."

I didn't like it, and she knew it. As we rode to the south camp little was said.

We pulled into their camp an hour or so before sundown and found the family at supper.

The man rose and came over to the wagon.

"Mister," I said, "I didn't get your name when I was out here this afternoon but I'd like to have you meet the owner of the J-B Ranch."

"You were too busy ordering me off to have asked, but it's Seth Blalock."

"Mr. Blalock, this here is Mrs. Bailey and my name is Will Jackson."

Blalock removed his hat and said he was pleased to meet Clatilda and wished it might be under better circumstances.

"Mr. Blalock," Clatilda said, "I understand you have an injured child."

"Yes'm, our little Daniel fell and broke his leg this afternoon, and he's in some pain right now. He can't even eat and you know for a six-year-old boy, he's got to be hurting a lot not to eat."

"May I see him, Mr. Blalock? It's possible I could help."

"My Annie has worked with him all afternoon and she's right good with kids. But, you're welcome to see what you can do."

Clatilda made William comfortable in a basket she'd brought for that purpose and stepped down from the buckboard.

Blalock introduced her to his wife, and they both left the table to go to the boy's bed. Shortly, Clatilda left the boy's bed and returned to the buckboard for a small leather satchel she'd brought. She took some hot water from a kettle on the fire and mixed a tea using a packet from the satchel. Then she and Mrs. Blalock raised the boy's head so that he might drink. They then sat down beside the boy's bed and commenced to chat.

As for me, I sat in the buggy while Blalock had gone back to his supper. I felt about as welcome as a preacher in a saloon.

It was almost an hour before Clatilda and Mrs. Blalock arose and came back to tell Blalock what had been done. It seemed the boy was easy and had, in fact, gone to sleep. Both Blalock and his wife escorted Clatilda to the buckboard, thanking her profusely but neither Blalock, nor his wife said a word to me.

We headed back to the ranch and had gone a mile or so before anything was said.

"They seem nice enough people, Will," Clatilda said, rather quietly.

"Nice enough to give one hundred and sixty acres of your land?"

"Oh, Will, I just don't know. Ann Blalock seems such a gentle person, and they have invested everything they have in this move. They were driven out of Kansas by drought and grasshoppers. She says this is their last hope. After they gave that Johnson person the money for their homestead; they have only a few dollars left."

"You mean they paid Johnson for their land?"

"No, she said they had to pay him one dollar an acre to file the homestead claim for them."

"Then, for sure, this Johnson's a crook. Ma'am, you don't have to pay to file on a homestead. You just have to 'prove up'. That means you plant a crop or run cattle and build a home. There's probably more, but I know you don't have to pay anyone to file."

"Oh, Will, I don't know how they will survive if they've lost their money and have no land either."

"Ma'am, I feel sorry for them, too, but I don't know what can be done. They must either be put off your ranch or you're going to buy yourself the kind of headache that will last forever."

She said little more, all the way back to the house. She did not offer dinner nor did I ask. I think the air around her table that evening would have been a little cool to enjoy.

I carried the milk pails to the house that next morning not really knowing what to expect. When I knocked, the door opened immediately and Clatilda stood there with a grand smile on her face.

"I've got it all worked out! Come in and let me explain."

To say I was taken aback would have been an understatement.

"Will, do you know that flat ground, north of the barn running east to the big pines?"

"Yes. I'd thought about using it to calve on next spring."

"Well, would you say there's at least a hundred and fifty acres there?"

"No, ma'am, I'd say closer to two-fifty, maybe three hundred."

"So much the better. What would you say if I told you I'm thinking of selling that piece of ground to the Blalocks?"

"I'd say it's your land, ma'am, and whatever you chose to do with it suits me."

She stood for a moment and looked at me in that direct way of hers. Then she stepped to the stove and dished up my breakfast which she sat before me without a comment. I waited for her to sit down with her plate so that she might bless the food, which was her practice.

She went to a side table and began sifting flour on a mound of dough she had there. I waited a moment then quietly blessed my food and set to eating.

Clatilda turned from kneading the dough, folded her arms and leaned back against the table.

"Will Jackson, I'll not have this!"

"Ma'am, I don't know what you're talking about."

"Oh, yes you do. You're smart enough and sensitive enough to know exactly what I'm talking about. If you have a problem with selling that land to the Blalocks, let's talk about it."

"Ma'am, I have no right to say anything. As a hired hand, I feel privileged you even told me of your intent. But as that same hired hand, it is not my right to comment, other than favorably upon your decisions."

She stood there for a moment leveling her gaze at me. She then turned back to kneading her dough.

Still with her back to me she said, "Will, I need flour. Will you, please, hitch the buckboard and go into John Terry's and bring four hundred pounds? We will talk more when you return."

Chapter 19

I hitched up the buckboard but I fought with myself all the time I was doing it, for I fully expected to be let go when I got back from the settlement. I don't like to see anyone sent packing, least of all, me. I argued with myself halfway to town about just going back and drawing my time but I figured nightfall would find me on the way to Texas, one way or the other, so why hurry.

When I had loaded the flour, I realized Clatilda had not given me money to pay John Terry. I offered to pay out of my own pocket but John said not to worry. Mrs. Bailey had more credit at his store than she would probably ever use. That puzzled me, but I let it go.

All the way back to the ranch, I swore at and about homesteaders, settlers, squatters and even some at myself and other cross-grained fools.

I carried the four sacks of flour into the back storage room of the cabin without a word being said. When I completed that task, Clatilda asked me to put up the horses and come back to the cabin. While in the barn, I saddled my pony and rolled my bedroll, tying it on my saddle.

When I returned to the cabin, Clatilda had a piece of apple pie with heavy cream on top and a steaming cup of coffee sitting at my place at the table.

"Sit down, please Will, we must talk."

She seated herself across from me. She had nothing in front of her except a closed tablet, quill pen and a jar of ink.

"Will, I came very close, this morning, to asking you to leave."

"I know, ma'am and. . . . ."

"Please, don't interrupt, Will. I have thought and prayed about this matter and I've settled, in my heart and mind what I must do. Please let me get it all out then we will discuss it."

"Yes, ma'am."

"As you know, so well, I cannot run this ranch alone. I could hire John Terry's son, if I chose to have a youth whom I would have, daily, to give detailed instructions. I could be taken in marriage by Brother Glaston or probably one or two others and I would then give over to my husband the management of my affairs. I chose to do neither of these things. Will, there are no unmarried men, of my age, of my faith, in this area. As I have told you, I chose not to be in a polygamous marriage; therefore, that is out of the question. So what do I do? I thought I had no problems until you up and disagreed on the solution to the problem presented by the Blalocks. Normally a sister in my position would submit her problems to her Bishop for his advice but as I've told you and Bishop Terry, I will deal with my affairs myself. Will, I have thought long and hard about what I am about to say to you, and I wish you to know beforehand, I want your truthfulness more than anything else. May I expect that—unqualified truth?"

"Yes, ma'am, I guess I don't rightfully know any other way."

She looked at me a moment, then opened the tablet lying in front of her.

"Will, I have two offers to make to you. You may choose either one or neither. Also, I would ask, after your decision, if you choose one or the other, that we discuss all of the pros and cons of the Blalock problem."

"That's fair enough, ma'am."

"All right, Will, hang onto your hat. I'm afraid you're in for somewhat of a surprise. Please don't stop me until I have presented both offers."

I felt like I should run out and jump on my horse and ride off in all directions at once. I knew not what to expect. But, I had no anticipation of being too happy with any part of what was to be presented and least of all choosing between any of those options.

"First, Will, I have written out an agreement that makes you a full partner in this ranch. You assume one half of its obligations and would automatically own one half of its assets. I can tell you the ranch has no obligations and considerable assets. The only exclusion would be my forty-five percent interest in John Terry's general store and the money I have in his safe. I have considerable cash hidden here in the cabin which would be made available to you for ranch expenses. All future profits would be divided equally between you and me. I would split my share, eventually with William."

"But, ma'am…"

"Please, Will, wait. This is as sensitive for me as it is for you."

I sat and watched as she closed the tablet and, visibly, took a long deep breath.

"The second offer is as difficult for me to make as it will be for you to hear. My other offer, Will, is my hand in marriage."

Well, right then I absolutely panicked. It must have shown on my face, for Clatilda blanched, stopped talking and stared at her hands, lying on the tablet.

"Will," she finally began again, "I do not wish to frighten you but I guess all I might be able to make you understand is that I feel I cannot, possibly, run this ranch. Furthermore, as strange as it may seem, I don't want to. I am willing to marry you even though I believe such a marriage, at this time, will be difficult. I am not concerned about anything or anyone else but the two of us and William. But, I can see problems you may not even understand at this time. However, my respect and trust obligate me to present this to you."

We then both sat there in silence for what seemed a long time. She spoke first.

"Obviously, Will, there is the third alternative, and that is that you will reject both offers."

"Clatilda, please understand that I believe I know what a sacrifice you are proposing to make, but I have just one question. Do you want to keep this ranch so badly?"

"Oh, no, Will! Like most material things, I will nurture and protect what I have, but I will not allow them to dictate my life. What I am trying to say, is that I don't care to keep this ranch if you will not stay. Should you choose to reject both offers, I will probably sell the land and livestock and move to town and participate in operating the General Store."

I sat there for a moment staring at the table. I was overwhelmed and more than a little excited.

"Will, I would like to tell you to think this over for a few days, but I'm afraid I have need of an answer now."

"I have no problem with giving you an answer now. It's just that my answer does not lie with either of the three options you have given me. I will say that I do not care to leave and as we agreed before, I will stay until you ask me to leave. As for the two offers. First, I cannot and will not accept your gift, given the sacrifice on your part, not withstanding the fact that, in my opinion, William is entitled to one-third, at least. So, if you kept your fair share, you have but a third, not half of a half to give away. As far as your second offer, Clatilda, my admiration for you is great. I respect and trust you absolutely. Am I willing to marry you? Not just to provide you with steady help on your ranch."

"No, Will, that's not the way I meant . . . ."

"Now, you listen, ma'am. I need to have my say. I will stay on this ranch as long as you will have me. I may occasionally disagree with you on how to run it, but I'll try to act, in the future, a little less like a baby and a lot more serious about our disagreement. Now, please, tear up that contract, deed or whatever it is, put away your wedding dress, for now, and let's discuss the Blalock problem."

She had looked sharply at me when I had added the 'for now' to putting away her wedding dress. She gazed at me for a moment longer then stepped to the stove and poured me another cup of coffee.

"Ma'am, do many of you Mormons drink coffee?"

"No, I believe I can say mine is the only home of our ward in which coffee may be found."

"Well, then, I'm going to tell you something, and I'm going to ask you something."

"Clatilda, you are probably the best cook I've ever seen, but you can't brew coffee to save yourself. Also, I am uncomfortable with you being the only Mormon in this valley with coffee in your home. Please throw it out, and I will do without it. It won't kill me."

She stood for a moment.

"Will, I hope I did not offend you with my 'offers'. I would not, for the world."

"No, ma'am, but we'd better get on with this Blalock thing."

"Why are you so set against selling the Blalock's land we don't really need anyway?"

"Really only two reasons. One, I've already ordered them off J-B land and the second; how do you expect them to pay? Surely you don't intend to give them the land."

"Should we offer the land, we could let them work it off."

"Doing what?"

"Well, I've noticed there always seems to be more work completed by Monday morning than was done by Saturday at supper time. Are you working nights, Will?"

I had no answer. I just looked at her. She looked back at me, then just as bold as brass winked at me. I almost fell out of my chair.

I answered, "I don't think Blalock could ever pay for that many acres of ground just by doing what little work I might do on any Sunday."

"Are you willing to talk about it with him?"

"Yeah, but what if he's already gone?"

"Somehow, I don't believe he will be. Why don't you go hitch up the buckboard, and we'll go find out?"

Chapter 20

Sure enough, we found the Blalocks still there. A small girl was playing a game with blocks on Daniel's bed. He was sitting up, apparently feeling much better.

Blalock and his wife both welcomed Clatilda as a friend. Neither spoke to me.

Clatilda sat in the buckboard, holding William in her lap.

"Mr. Blalock, my ranch foreman has something he wants to talk with you about. He speaks for me."

"We ain't leaving, if that's what you're here to say. And, friend, was I you, I wouldn't be bringing no ladies or babies with me, when you try to run me off."

"Oh, shut up Blalock, or I'll forget what I came for and the next time you see me you'd better be looking over your shoulder as you leave!"

"Be still, Seth," said Mrs. Blalock, "at least hear him out."

"Blalock, you are not going to homestead this piece of land. That's final and the end of it."

I stopped and looked at him. He looked right back. I'll say this; there was no give in the man.

"There's just one question I have before we go on. Are you a good worker?"

"I worked for everything I ever had, friend. Sometimes things have gone wrong, but there's two things I gave up a long time ago. One's crying over spilt milk, and the other being afraid of anything or anyone."

As I sat there with the reins of the buggy team in my hand, I felt this was probably a man I would like to know. But, there was this wall that had grown between us—built by my demands that he leave and his refusal to do so. It took conscious will on my part not to slap the team and leave that place.

"Blalock, do you have just the two children?"

"Not that it's any of your business, but no, we have an older boy. He's fishing down by the creek."

"Can you call him up here and let him mind your other two? I've something I want to show you and your wife."

"Anything you have to say to me, say now and here."

"Man, I'm trying to deal with you so you're not too badly hurt. But, believe me, you're making it tough!"

He said not another word, just walked to the back of his wagon and whistled sharply. A boy of twelve or thirteen came trotting to the wagon. Blalock had a brief discussion with the boy, then came back to the wagon.

"You hold my baby, Annie, while I get in the back. I had Will put this back seat on for us in case you folks decided to come." Clatilda said as she stepped on the wheel rim then easily back into the buckboard's second seat. Blalock helped his wife up after she had given William back to Clatilda.

I said nothing more, just turned the team and headed back toward the barn. The women chatted constantly along the way.

We circled the barn, crossed the creek, which down valley ran by Blalock's wagon, then came out on flat ground.

I pulled the buckboard up on a slight knoll by the creek.

"How does this land look to you?" I ask Blalock.

"It seems good looking land. So what?"

"The 'so what' is that my boss is fixing to offer you this land if you're a mind to own it and a way can be found for you to pay for it."

"I won't be wanting this land. If you'd give Annie and me a ride back to our camp, we'd be obliged."

I turned and looked at him where he sat, rigid as steel and staring straight ahead.

"Step down with me, Blalock. Let's you and me take a walk up stream a ways."

He looked at me right sharp, and I thought for a moment he would refuse. Then with one movement he stepped down and came around beside me. We walked a couple of hundred feet up the creek bank and stopped in a grove of cottonwood trees.

"Now, mister, I'm going to say a couple of things, then if you want to go back to your camp, I'll take you."

"Be careful, friend." was all he said.

"Blalock, your Annie told Mrs. Bailey about Kansas and about your giving that crook in Alamosa most of your cash money. So, the fact you are in temporary hard times is known and doesn't matter. Mrs. Bailey has told me that if you want this land, somewhere about three hundred acres, she is prepared to sell it to you, and you can pay for it by working it out."

He stood, staring at his feet for a couple of minutes.

"Jackson, you got to know you're offering me a way out of a mess I'd be a fool not to take. But I don't see how I could ever pay, in labor, what this place is worth. What are you asking for it?"

"To begin with, all the work I do on Sundays."

He just looked at me with a blank stare.

"Oh, don't worry about that. That's a joke between Mrs. Bailey and me."

"I'm serious," he said, "what work do you have in mind?"

"Let's go back to the wagon, and you can talk about that with Mrs. Bailey."

"I thought she said you could speak for her. I'm some uncomfortable dealing with a woman."

"Don't let this woman bother you, mister. She's got a heart as soft and gentle as goose down, but the mind of a banker. Just watch yourself."

He looked over at me as we walked back to the wagon. "You

ain't Mormon are you?"

"No, I'm not. Why?"

"Is she?"

"Yeah, she's the widow of one of twelve Mormon men who settled this valley."

"Are Mormons anywhere as crooked to deal with as people in Alamosa told us?"

"I've found the ones I've dealt with to be as honest as hard working mules. But, they flat will not be pushed around. I guess they had all of that they will stand for, a few years back, in the East."

He said no more but when we came up to the wagon, he stepped over to his wife's side.

"Annie, they're offering to sell us this land, and allowing me to work out the cost."

"Can you do that, Seth and still work the land and build our home?"

"I don't know. I'm fixing on talking that out with Mrs. Bailey. Do you like the land, Annie?"

"Yes, even better than our place in Kansas."

Blalock stood and looked at his wife for a moment, then turned to Clatilda.

"Ma'am, I am much obliged to you for your offer and would like nothing better than to take you up on it. But, I just don't see how I could do anything acceptable to you to pay for it."

"Mr. Blalock, are you a good farmer?"

"I believe I am, ma'am."

"Have you ever raised potatoes?"

"Of course! Before we were dried out in Kansas I raised an acre every year for our own use and I usually had two or three hundred pounds to sell."

"Could you raise a hundred acres of potatoes, Mr. Blalock?"

"I probably could, ma'am, but that would leave me with practically no time to work off my debt to you."

"Would you be willing to raise potatoes on this land and give me half of what you raise as your annual payment for this land?"

"Why, sure. But there are two problems. First off I don't have money to buy seed potatoes and what's more, I don't think my family could eat all the potatoes that could be raised on fifty acres."

"Are those the only problems you have with my proposition, sir?"

"Those are pretty good sized problems, ma'am. But, yes I guess those are my only real concerns."

"All right, Mr. Blalock. I have the ability to obtain seed potatoes and also I can provide a market for all or part of your fifty acres of potatoes."

Blalock stood there for a moment. He looked long at his wife. Then he walked around the wagon and stood looking at that flat meadow for a few more minutes before he said anything.

"Mrs. Bailey, if you will fix up some kind of contract, I expect we could get moved up here tomorrow morning."

"Tonight!" I said.

He jerked around to look directly at me.

"Why tonight, my friend? Isn't tomorrow soon enough?"

"No. I will come down to help you, but it will be tonight."

He looked at me then broke into a big grin.

"You're going to have your way, even if it makes the sun come up out of the West, ain't you, Jackson?"

"I keep my word; no matter who I give it to. And, I don't back up much."

"Is that all right with you, Mrs. Bailey? It'll mean we'll have to settle the details tomorrow."

"I don't see twelve hours, or even twelve days, making that much difference."

"Then, let's do it, Jackson if you'll have us back to our camp, I think we can get up here by dark."

Chapter 21

We didn't quite make it by dark, but the Blalocks were settled in before moon rise. When they were all set, I went to the barn and after milking, took the pails to the house.

My knock was answered immediately.

"Are our new neighbors all settled?" Clatilda asked as I placed the milk on the table.

I turned to see her dishing up stew and setting a fresh loaf of bread on the table.

"Ma'am, you knew all along, didn't you?"

She turned and looked straight at me for a moment.

"Yes, Will, I told you I had thought and prayed about this. John Terry and I have talked about this some. The idea of having someone grow potatoes as a cash crop has many good aspects that are good for our community."

"Very well, then."

I finished my supper and went to bed. The next morning I had breakfast and left to check the cattle. I found where Jethro had fashioned a wooden shuttle gate on the east creek for irrigating his hay. After I'd returned to the barn for a shovel, I opened the "gate" in the river bank and watched as life-giving water spread out and over the two nearest hay fields. I waited until both fields were covered then, with rocks and dirt, closed off the creeks flow into the fields.

By the time I closed off the creek it was coming on to dusk, and I was hungry. I rode to the barn and put up my horse and the shovel. I was just finishing my milking chores when Clatilda stepped into the barn.

"I was a little concerned about you, Will, when you didn't come in for lunch."

"I was busy irrigating, and time just got away from me. I'll be through here in a couple of minutes."

She said nothing more, just turned and went to the house.

I walked in to find my supper on the table, piping hot. Clatilda was seated at the table with her hands folded in her lap. As I sat down she blessed the food then looked up at me.

"We waited for you this morning. I thought you might have wanted to be here when I consummated the sale."

"No, ma'am, I figured you had that all thought out, too. So, I didn't think there was much I could add."

She sat quietly in thought the rest of the meal. When we had finished, I pushed back my chair to rise.

"Will, if you have started irrigating and what with branding coming up next week, I had better start packing you a dinner so you don't have to stop to come to the house at noon. I remember many days when Jethro could not do so during this time of year."

"That will be good, ma'am," I said as I stood and left for the barn and my bed.

Days, and then weeks began to fly by. First there was the branding. I had plenty of help . Good help I might add and the ladies seemed to enjoy their brush arbor. Many left saying they were coming back when their husband helped with the haying. During the two weeks I worked around the valley that summer helping others hay, I got to know the settlers much better. I found that, like any other group of folks, there were some I took to and others I didn't want to have much to do with. But, the one thing true about them all was that they were hard workers. There was this one old boy; Jesse Turner was his name. He must have been in his sixties. He and I were hauling hay to his barn one afternoon when one of the horses was spooked by a squirrel in the grass and hauled off and kicked Turner on the side of his hip, right behind his front overall pocket. It knocked him down, and I thought for sure he had to be bad hurt.

I ran over to check to see how badly injured he was but by the time I got to him, he was already on his feet again. He dropped his overalls and examined himself. He had a bruise the size of a pie plate but the skin was not broken, and he said he didn't think any bones were broken either. I figured he'd go to the house and spend the next few days in bed. That old man darned near worked me into the ground that same afternoon. Then, when we had unloaded the last of the hay, he wanted to know if I had time to go fishing with him. He said he had a hankering for fresh-caught fish that night. I begged off and headed home. Went to sleep in the saddle twice along the way.

Chapter 22

The summer went by quickly, so quickly that I was surprised to see, one evening, that the leaves on some of the quakies, up on the mountainside were turning a golden yellow. There was still much I needed to do before winter. As I rode in that evening, I noticed a buggy and two saddle horses tied to the rail in front of the barn. I was curious but went ahead and did my chores. When I finished milking, I started to wait until Clatilda's guests had left but then for some reason I went ahead and knocked on the cabin door. The door was opened by Bishop Terry.

"Come in, Mr. Jackson. We were hoping you'd get in before we had to leave. I've a couple of things I'd like to talk to you about."

I stepped in and sat the milk in its usual place and turned to face the three men. Bishop Terry then introduced the two men as his counselors in what he called his Bishopric.

The one man he introduced as Jim Burk and the other was my friend, Jess Turner.

We chatted a little about Turner's hip which he insisted had not caused him a bit of trouble.

Bishop Terry said, "Mr. Jackson, we understand you and Mrs. Bailey have had a bit of trouble with homesteaders."

"Not really. We had some folks that wanted to homestead across the east creek. Two families, in fact. Neither family stayed there!"

He looked at me strangely. "Yes, we understand one is now farming three hundred acres north of the creek behind your barn."

When I didn't respond, he looked at Clatilda then back to me.

"Mr. Jackson, I'm not sure you are aware of it, but Jethro Bailey signed a pact when we, the first twelve families, came into this valley. We agreed not to sell any land except to another saint. It appears Mrs. Bailey has violated that pact."

"Bishop Terry, what you're talking about is really not my business. I'm a hired hand and so far as that goes I have naught to say beyond what Mrs. Bailey has already told you."

"Well, I really have one question of you, Mr. Jackson. Do you think you could get this second set of squatters to leave as easily as the first?"

I stood there with one hand on the table and the other hooked in my pocket. I looked over and Clatilda was looking at me with almost a pleading on her face.

"Ma'am, did you tell these people the whole deal?"

"Yes, I did, Will."

"Then no, Bishop Terry, I'll not help you run these folks off what they have been told was their ground."

"Well then, Mr. Jackson, we really have a problem."

"Why do you have such a problem?"

"The pact signed by Mrs. Bailey's late husband. It's binding on all of us, and we depended on it."

"Bishop, I'd like to ask you something. I don't know about your pact and as far as I'm concerned, I don't need to. But, what I want to know is, do you understand the whole deal Mrs. Bailey has with the Blalocks?"

"Yes, I believe she explained it quite thoroughly."

I glanced over at Clatilda. She nodded her head.

"Then, what I'd like to ask you, Bishop, is: do you have anyone in your group that wishes to trade places with the Blalocks?"

The question took him aback. He stood for a moment looking at the floor then at Clatilda and finally faced me.

"No, Mr. Jackson, I don't believe I do."

"Well, then, let me ask you one more thing. Is your church prepared to buy that three hundred acres?"

"Not hardly, but there is the matter of the pact."

"What good is the pact if no one wants to do what it says. I think you'll find that what Mrs. Bailey proposes will benefit the entire area. What's more, Bishop, outside of cattle and hay, I'd be surprised if any crop besides potatoes could be grown up there, what with the weather and seeing how high up that ground is."

"You know, Bishop," spoke up Turner, "I believe Mr. Jackson

may have a point. It could be the best way to settle this whole thing is to arrange to have the Blalock's taught the gospel. Bring the mountain to Mohammed, as the case may be."

I didn't know what Turner meant about that mountain stuff, but Bishop Terry agreed almost too readily. They apologized to Clatilda, if they had upset her, shook hands all around and left almost as fast as the telling.

Clatilda went to the stove and was stirring up the fire when I returned from seeing the men away.

"I'm sorry you were put through that, Will," she said turning to face me.

"Ma'am, there is no problem. I just hope I didn't upset your Bishop."

"No, I don't believe you did. Your views of the problem were to the point. I believe you offered us all a way out of a bad situation."

We then enjoyed the most relaxed meal we'd had in weeks. We discussed the work on the ranch, and I suggested not selling off any of the cattle that year. We had over seventy new calves and plenty of hay to carry the herd over, even in a hard winter. She said Blalock had told her he would be ready to harvest his first crop of potatoes in ten days to two weeks and would need help. We discussed whether to ask the men in her church to help or hire some of the young men and boys from the settlement. Upon my advice she agreed to hire young men. She suggested I might want to discuss the opportunity at the men's meeting that next Sunday. When she said this, I looked at her and her expression was as bland as boiled milk.

"Ma'am, you're doing it again, aren't you?"

She said not a word. Just stood and took a big fat berry pie from the warming oven atop her stove. She sliced the pie into four pieces and gave me a slice with cream atop.

"Clatilda, tell me something. Just how far have you gone with your plans for me?"

She looked at me for a moment, then winked.

While she turned to replace the pie in the warming oven, I sat there wondering where I would be if I'd gone on to Texas earlier last winter.

Chapter 23

There was no more said on the matter and, Sunday, we went to church. First I went to the men's meeting, which they referred to as "Priesthood Meeting" and then we whiled away the afternoon on the church grounds. Clatilda had a meal in a basket and between enjoying the warm autumn afternoon and playing with William, time passed quickly. During the afternoon I did notice the women of some of the families, enjoying the afternoon as we were, glancing long and frequently at both of us.

As we were leaving the afternoon services, Bishop Terry asked Clatilda if she would stay a moment as he wished to talk to her. I took William and went to hitch up the buggy which I then brought around to the front of the church to await Clatilda.

I didn't have long to wait before Clatilda and the Bishop came walking down the church steps. He accompanied her all the way to the buggy.

"Mr. Jackson, how do you enjoy our services?"

"Just fine, Bishop; what all I understand. I like the easy feeling of friendship everyone seems to have for each other."

"I've talked with Clatilda about a situation and, she says she will discuss it with you. If I can help, please let me know."

With that he turned and went back into the church.

"What was that all about?" I asked.

"Let's go on home. I'll feed William and put him to bed then we'd best have a talk."

Little was said on the way back to the ranch. I studied on what it could be about. All that time, I had a nagging feeling in the back of my mind that I knew exactly what it was all about.

I was sitting at the table working on my tally book when Clatilda came in from putting William to bed. She got us each a glass of milk and some bread and cheese.

"What now?" I asked.

"Bishop Terry says some of the members are questioning our relationship. I thought that by bringing you to church there might be a developing friendship that would allay any suspicions some seem to have. It hasn't worked. What's more, some believe your interest in the church is not sincere."

"I've not thought about having any 'interest' in your church. I've only gone when you asked and then only to conduct the business of the ranch."

"Do you not like our church?"

"I never said that. What I know of what you people believe, I like. What you believe in a churchy way, I can't honestly say I understand. I'll say this: over the past few years I've heard a lot about Mormons, mostly bad, very bad. I have found nothing said to me in the past supported by what I've come to know of your people."

"Would you feel more comfortable discussing our beliefs with Bishop Terry?"

"Is it possible to have the same discussion with Jess Turner?"

"Yes, if you wish."

"Then, if you'll give me a day off this week, I'll ride over and maybe go fishing with Jess."

"Go when you please and take all the time you'll need. Maybe William and I will go as far as the store with you. I have some things I need."

So it was that I came to spend Wednesday of that week with Jess Turner. He started at the beginning and told me all about the Church. When he'd told most everything, he stopped, almost mid-sentence, and asked me flat out if I was ready to be baptized and join their church. I told him not yet but I was going to think over everything he had told me. I left, Jess at his dooryard. I was a wiser man with a nice string of fish.

I stopped by the store to find that Clatilda had already left. I rode on out to the ranch, stabled my horse, and began my chores. I was deep in thought, milking the cow when Clatilda came into the barn.

"Did you find out what you needed to know?" she asked.

"Mostly. At least I found what I believe has been bothering me when I read your Book of Mormon. I aim to test my theory tonight."

"Mind telling me what it is?"

"Let me make sure I'm right. If I am, I'll let you know at breakfast."

Clatilda had my breakfast on the table, the next morning when I brought in the milk. Before I could seat myself, however, she wanted to know what I'd found out about the Book of Mormon. Just like that! It was as if she had waited all night to ask that one question.

"Well, I found out one thing for certain. I should have started at the end and read back."

"If I had started at the end of the Book of Moroni, I would have known what Jess told me. I mentioned to him the problem I was having and his only suggestion was that I continue to prayerfully read. That's what I'd not been doing. So, last night, I prayed. I finished the book last night and found, in the end of Moroni, the part about praying to see if the book is true."

"Well?" she said, leaning forward.

"Well, yes, it made everything much easier."

"Well?" she repeated.

"Well, what?"

"Well, do you believe the Book of Mormon to be true?" Now she demanded.

"Of course."

"Just that! Of course?"

"There is one thing, I would like to read it again now that I know how to get the most of it."

"You keep it as long as you wish," she said. "It is my pleasure to lend it to you."

Chapter 24

Clatilda had arranged for seven boys and young men to help in the potato harvest while she had been at the store that day. She also wanted me to work with Blalock and the boys.

She seemed rather nervous that evening about something and short of coming right out and asking there was no way to know why.

As we were finishing supper, she asked an unusual question.

"Will, have you ever raised goats?"

"No ma'am, I haven't raised sheep either. Don't figure to. Why?"

"There was a man in the store, this afternoon. He had a whole wagon load of goats. There must have been twenty-five or thirty. He wanted to sell them all for fifty cents each. I was tempted. My father kept goats while I was growing up. I personally never cared for the milk, but you can make delicious cheese from it. And, goats are really no trouble."

"When's that man bringing your goats out here?"

"Will Jackson, you can be the most exasperating man in the world! How did you know I'd bought the goats?"

"I believe Jess said something about 'the keys of discernment'. How's that for a four-bit word?"

"I can see Brother Turner, in the future, is going to have to be given less access to you."

Chuckling as she did so, she stepped to the warming oven and produced a berry cobbler.

"We'd better enjoy this. I heard today they have already had a killing frost in the high country. Pretty soon, it'll be back to dried apricot pies."

"I don't know whether I can put up with that. I'll just have to get by."

Digging and sacking those potatoes proved to be more hard, backbreaking work than I had done in a while. It took almost three weeks to complete. At that, we left some in the ground, frozen by a ten-inch wet snow and a hard freeze the following week. We would not have been able to ever finish had not Blalock rigged up a harrow type device that scooped the potatoes to the top of the ground. We still had to pick up the potatoes and pack them. It was hard work, but we wound up with almost seven thousand bushels off the three hundred acres. Blalock said he could do better the next year if I would turn the herd in on his property for part of the time I was feeding hay. He offered to haul the hay; he and his boy. He said the fertilizer he would gain could maybe increase his yield by as much as a third. I told him to plan on it and as soon as he was ready to begin hauling hay.

We had scoured the countryside for all sizes of baskets. We wound up with potatoes in everything from sewing baskets to wicker laundry baskets. Clatilda finally had John Terry get three thousand tow sacks from Pueblo. Those burlap bags each held one hundred pounds which made distribution easier. We arranged, with a broker, to have all three thousand sacks shipped to Pueblo. He paid John Terry upon receipt. The rest were sold to those living in the valley. When Clatilda and I went to the Blalocks cabin to settle up, I thought Annie Blalock would never stop bawling.

Seth was prepared to give Clatilda his entire share, as payment on the property; in addition to her half. She refused saying she would only take her half. And he should keep the rest for his family. He sat and stared at what was left on that table.

"You know," he said, "I had about half this much hard cash when we left Ohio for Kansas. And, that was after selling everything we could not get in our wagon or tie on behind. And, now I'm getting two hundred acres, a market for my produce and good neighbors. See, Will, I told you I don't run easy!"

"Yeah, but you ain't astraddle that creek either!"

"You're a hard man, Will Jackson, but we like you in spite of it!" Annie said. I guess I turned red from my collar to my hair line. At least everyone had a good laugh.

Chapter 25

When we got back to the house that cold blustery afternoon, after settling with the Blalocks, there were two men squatted down on the lee side of the barn, smoking and holding their horses' reins.

My Texas upbringing got the best of me.

"Who are you two, and who was it gave you permission to step down in our door yard?"

They both stood and stepped around their horses.

"Are you Jethro Bailey?" asked one. He was sort of short and stocky. He had, at least, removed his hat to reveal a shock of the whitest hair I'd ever seen.

Before Clatilda could say anything, I responded.

"Who's asking, and why do you want to know?"

"We're U.S. Marshals, and we've got a warrant for your arrest for bigamous marriage. We have it on good information you have two wives. We'll have to take you in to the territorial court over to Salt Lake City. Get your clothes or whatever you need, we will go on back to the settlement tonight."

"Mister, I ain't going anywhere with you, now or ever."

"Bailey, I don't want any trouble with you, man. If you don't come peaceably, we'll put you in irons, and I guarantee you'll come then."

"You have two problems, friend. First off, Jethro Bailey lies halfway up that east hill beside his wife, Jennifer. Both, long dead, for almost a year. Second, I don't want you here. So, git!"

They looked, one at the other then the white-haired one spoke again.

"If you're not Jethro Bailey, what right do you have running settlers off their homestead?"

"Now, we come down to it! Did Tim Johnson send you?"

"Don't matter who sent us. Just answer my questions!"

While he'd been talking he and his partner had been standing on the near, or left side of my horse, I quietly slipped my pistol from my holster and held it down against my right leg.

I eased the hammer back and laid the cocked pistol atop my saddle horn.

"Fellows, I don't care if you're U. S. Marshals or what, I want you off this ranch and right now."

"Son," said the white-haired marshal, "you got any idea what kind of trouble you could get into, pulling down on a U.S. Marshal?"

Clatilda had nudged the reins and the buggy began moving off to the side.

"Lady," said the other man, "you just hold that buggy still, if you know what's good for you."

"All right! That tears it!" I said, "you two both drop your gun belts and step away from those horses. Do it now!"

Both quickly dropped their guns and stepped back. But the younger one kept hold of the reins from both animals.

"Drop those reins, and right now!"

"But, mister," he said, "if I do they might spook and run off!"

"If you're dumb enough not to train your pony to stand ground-hitched, then you ought to have to chase him."

He dropped the reins and, sure enough, both animals shied away eight or ten feet. I stepped off my horse and walked over removing both rifles from the horses. I then turned to the men.

"You can pick up your pistols and rifles at John Terry's store in the settlement, next Monday."

"Next Monday," the white-haired one said, stepping forward, "we're due back in Alamosa day after tomorrow. You'd better not make me have to ride all the way back here for my guns."

"I've got a question for you friend. How did you figure to get me all the way into Utah territory then be back in Alamosa by day after tomorrow?"

"That's none of your affair, mister. It's enough that you understand you're in deep trouble."

"Now, both of you, I'm going to tell you something. You go tell

Johnson, his sandy didn't work. Either one of them. The homesteaders or you two. One more thing; I ever see you, your friend or that Tim Johnson on this ranch, I'll shoot you all on sight."

"Huh," said the younger of the two, "I thought all you Mormons were the 'turn the other cheek' kind."

"I ain't Mormon, yet. I come from down in the Panhandle country. The fellow you're dealing with now is all Texas, and I never turn the other cheek. Now, you fellows better be getting on your way. Those two ponies are getting farther and farther away!"

They looked over to see the horses now thirty or forty feet away and walking toward the settlement.

"Will, I am concerned," said Clatilda.

"Ma'am there's no need to worry. It was plain they were planning to scare your husband so he wouldn't run off homesteaders. Too much of what they said was too thin and too connected to Johnson."

She went to the house while I put up the horses and her buggy. After I'd milked I went on to the house. While I was setting the milk on a table, she turned from the stove.

"So, you're 'all Texas' and never turn the other cheek?"

I looked sharply at her to find a big grin on her face.

"Seriously, Will, do you think you might have handled the situation differently?"

"Would you have had me allow them to tell you where you could go; and you in your own door yard?"

"No, but taking their guns? What would you have done if they refused?"

"What do you think I should have done?"

"I've been studying about that all the time you were doing your chores. I really don't like your doing it, but I'm troubled trying to fault you. One other thing, Will, did you see any badge? I didn't."

"Nope, and that's another thing. I saw a U. S. Marshal pick up an old boy down to Amarillo once. He showed this man his badge, a little book of some kind and the warrant for the arrest. A U. S. Marshal, in this country has got to be a lot more savvy than those two. I doubt a real marshal would have allowed me to draw my pistol without challenge."

"Are you going to take those guns into the settlement tonight?"

"Absolutely not. I told them they could pick them up Monday. I'll give them to John Terry, Sunday after church."

"Are you going to services Sunday?"

"Yep."

"There's no ranch business to be taken care of, that I know."

I looked over at her. She had a little smile on her face and a glint dancing in her eyes.

"Clatilda, you're a lot of things, but you're not quite as sweet and innocent as you'd have me believe."

"You bet your boots, cowboy!" she said as she turned to the stove to dish up our meal.

Chapter 26

That Sunday morning Jess Turner took me under his arm and sat beside me in Priesthood Meeting. Once again, after the meeting, he ask me if I was ready to be baptized. Again I begged off, telling him I wanted a little more time to think it over.

That afternoon, we again had dinner at John Terry's home. I did not participate in any of the conversations and was frankly happy to go to the evening service and then head home.

It was long past dark when we reached the ranch, and Clatilda invited me in for a piece of pie and milk before I went to bed.

When I had stabled the team, I went back to the cabin. The door was opened immediately. Clatilda then stepped aside as I went in. There on the table was a large chocolate cake with one candle in its center.

"Happy Birthday, Will!"

I was flabbergasted. I looked at her, then at that layer cake. She must have been up at the crack of dawn to bake that cake before we went to church.

"Ma'am, how did you know today's my birthday?"

"Jess Turner told me."

"How would he have known?"

"He said you told him when and where you were born."

I thought again of that day on the river bank and the many things Jess and I talked of. "I probably did, we talked of so many things, I'm sure I probably told him that, also."

"Sit down, Will. William and I have a birthday present for you."

She went into the bedroom and returned with a big bulky package, all wrapped in colored paper. She handed it to me and said I should open it while she cut the cake and poured our milk.

When I opened the package, I could not believe my eyes. It was a sheepskin lined canvas coat. I slipped into it and turned up the shawl collar.

"Clatilda, I've often wanted one of these, but they are not easy to find and in the past, when I found one, I've always been short on cash."

"It seems the thing for you to have. I ordered it through the store. Had your birthday not been so convenient, it was my intent you should have it for this winter, anyway."

I didn't know what to say. I thanked her and left after I'd finished my piece of cake. I must confess I slept that night with my new sheepskin lined canvas coat pulled up over my shoulders.

Chapter 27

The next morning I stepped out of the barn into a snow storm. This was not going to be an early wet snow that would soon melt off. This was the real thing; the beginning of winter. I trudged to the house and knocked. Clatilda called for me to come on in. When I did, I found her, once again bathing William. She looked worn out.

"High fever, again?"

"Yes, I've been up all night trying to bring it down."

I felt of the child. He had a fever. Not too bad but he did have a fever.

"I'll go get you a bucket of cold water," I said.

"No need, I just brought one in a while ago."

"Have you been in and out in this storm all night?"

"I had no choice. I had to have cold water."

"Next time something like this happens, come get me up."

"I doubt that I'll do that; you need your sleep, too."

"Wonder why this always happens when it's snowing?"

We worked with the boy for another hour before his temperature seemed normal. He then went fast asleep and seemed fine.

Clatilda stirred up the stove and quickly prepared breakfast. I protested but she would have none of it. After breakfast, I made the same agreement I had with her, the last time William had required her to be up all night. I gathered some harness from the barn and William and I spent the morning; he sleeping and I working. Just before dinner time I heard Clatilda cough several times. It was about two, maybe two-thirty that afternoon, that she called me into her bedroom.

"Will, I am afraid we have trouble," she said as I walked into her room. "I feel that I am burning up, and I have this deep cough."

I placed the back of my hand to her forehead. It was hot to the touch.

"Clatilda, I'm afraid you caught yourself either a very bad cold, or the grippe, running in and out, last night."

"Please get a dish towel and tie it around William's mid-section so he can't get out of his crib then go get Mrs. Blalock. And, Will, please hurry!"

I grabbed a bridle and jumped on my pony and went tearing around the barn and up to the Blalocks. I was barely aware of the increased snowfall. I rode right up to their front door, jumped off my horse and banged on the door. It took but a minute for both Blalocks to answer.

"Why in the world are you banging on my door in this storm?" Blalock demanded.

I explained the problem to him and Annie, who had stepped to the door when she heard my voice.

"Seth, you hitch the wagon, and I'll gather some things. Will, tell Clatilda I'll be there as soon as I can."

When I walked into Clatilda's cabin, I could hear her deep cough. I looked in on her and was shocked by her appearance. She was pale as a ghost with red mottled splotches on both cheeks. Her eyes were glassy, in appearance, and she seemed lifeless except for the now ever more frequent fits of coughing.

It seemed I'd been back at the cabin only a few minutes when the Blalocks arrived. Annie Blalock went directly to the bedroom, closed the door and then all I heard was muffled conversation and Clatilda's coughing. Soon, Annie stuck her head out and told me to heat a couple of gallons of water and she told Seth to go home and bring back three woolen quilts they owned. She told me to find the bag of medications Clatilda had brought when she treated Blalock's boy, Daniel.

She was taking a kettle of hot water and Clatilda's bag as Seth came in with the three quilts.

"Will, I don't know how you are about praying, but it's something you might think strongly about doing. I'm afraid Clatilda has lung fever. I don't know a lot about it, but I do know it's often fatal."

She went back into Clatilda's room and closed the door leaving me standing there, astounded at how quickly Clatilda had become so seriously ill.

Seth and I sat at the table talking about little of consequence. It seemed both of us had an ear to the door of Clatilda's room. As the afternoon dragged on that door only opened twice and that for Annie, with little comment, to come for more hot water.

It was almost dark when Annie came out and said Clatilda wanted to see me.

I didn't know what to expect, but I was shocked to see Clatilda. To see Clatilda was seriously ill required only average eyesight. She was pale and drawn down fine as piano wire. There was now no color to her face at all, and she was wringing wet with sweat.

"Will, you must go to the settlement and bring Bishop and John Terry out here as fast as they can get here. Tell them I desperately need a blessing. Let them explain that to you. Please hurry, Will!"

I hurried. Bishop Terry happened to be in John Terry's store when I rode up. We were on our way back to the ranch in less than ten minutes. They didn't bother to explain what they were going to do, and I didn't ask.

When we got back to the cabin, the two men went directly into Clatilda's room. They asked Annie to step out and then they closed the door. We all sat around the kitchen table waiting and not saying much.

It was almost an hour before the door to Clatilda's bedroom opened.

"Mr. Jackson," said Bishop Terry, "Sister Clatilda will survive, we believe, but she is quite ill and will probably be so for sometime to come. You will need someone to be with her for a while. We will arrange for some of the sisters to help you."

"Sir, you will do nothing of the kind," spoke up Annie, "I will care for Mrs. Bailey and little William for as long as necessary."

"But, Mrs. Blalock," responded the bishop, "it could be a month or more before she's back on her feet."

Annie just looked the man straight in the eye for a long minute and finally when it was obvious she was waiting for him to say more and he wasn't going to, she said, "So?"

"But, Mrs. Blalock," the bishop began again, "you have your own family to care for."

"So? Sir you have no idea what this woman has done for me and my family nor will I share it with you. It's enough to say I will care for her for as long as such care is needed or even wanted. And, if, I care for her a year it will only begin to pay the interest on my family's debt of gratitude to Clatilda Bailey."

Bishop Terry stood and looked at Annie for a moment then asked her if she and her family had yet been visited by the "brethren?" When she answered no, he made a strange comment.

"Well, Mrs. Blalock, I hope you will receive them well. But, honestly I doubt they will teach you much you do not already know."

The two men left with my promise to come for them if Clatilda took a turn for the worse.

I went in to see Clatilda after the men had left. She looked as bad as she had earlier. But, she seemed much more calm and her spirits were definitely better. When I came back into the kitchen to get Clatilda a glass of cool water, Annie told me to come back after I'd given Clatilda the water; and we'd work out a schedule.

There was no "working out of a schedule." Annie Blalock told Seth and me what was going to be done. She would come down by seven each morning. I'd have to fend for myself for breakfast. She would prepare dinner for Seth, their children and me. Then before she left at five in the afternoon, she'd leave my supper in the warming oven. She said I was to bring my bedroll into the cabin and sleep by the fire.

When she had finished with the schedule, she looked me right in the eye. "And, Will Jackson, you see you take as good care of that fire and that sick lady as you do this ranch land."

From the time she made that statement until the day Seth and I lowered her into her grave, Annie Blalock was my friend.

The next three weeks were touch and go. Clatilda seemed to get a bit worse and I again went to the settlement for Bishop and John Terry. Once more they were with her for almost an hour. After their last visit, she began to improve, almost immediately.

It was just over nine weeks after Clatilda became ill when I was awakened one morning by someone shaking down the ashes in the kitchen stove. In a panic, thinking I had overslept, I jumped up from my pallet on the floor. Clatilda was standing at the stove with a skillet in one hand and a basket of eggs in the other.

"Good morning, sleepy head. How many eggs would you like for breakfast?"

I protested and tried to get her to go back to bed and wait for Annie. I was still protesting as I ate my eggs. Clatilda had a big breakfast herself.

When Annie came into the cabin, she jumped all over me, and right then! Clatilda defended me from the worst, but Annie stayed mad at me for a couple of days. She said if Clatilda had insisted on getting up, I should have, at least, cooked breakfast. I found out then that she did not yet know Clatilda quite as well as I did. I went on about my chores and checking the cattle, not returning to the cabin at noon. That evening when I came in, I passed Annie as she was leaving.

"Your supper's on the table. Probably cold by now!" was her greeting, farewell and general comment. She said not another word, just stepped upon the sleigh beside Seth and they headed home.

Whenever Annie had dished up my supper, it could have been only seconds before I came in, for steam was still rising from the food.

I looked in on Clatilda and found her sitting up in bed making lace. Her hands were flying, and I could tell she was some upset.

"Will," she said, not even looking up, "that Annie Blalock is a tyrant. She made me come back to bed and wouldn't let me get up all day!"

"Maybe she feels you're not ready to be up and about yet."

"Oh, I know. But, she won't let me do anything, and she orders me around as if I'm a child."

"She's taken care of you, this last two months, as if you were her own child, and her first born at that."

"Oh, I know, Will, but I have become so used to being the only woman in my kitchen, it irks me to be told what to do."

"Do you know what you sound like?"

"Yes, Will Jackson! I sound like some little crybaby! Now get on in there and eat your supper before it gets cold!"

Just as I finished my supper, I heard William start fussing and I turned toward his crib when Clatilda came out and took him. It was only moments before he was fast asleep. She came into the kitchen and went to her stove.

"This is what got me so fussed at today," she said, taking a big pie out of the warming oven.

She cut two generous pieces, added cream to their tops and sat one in front of me.

"Ma'am, what's a blessing?"

"Bishop Terry didn't explain it to you?"

"No, he didn't volunteer, and it was something you felt you needed. I was not obliged to get in the way. I figured there would be plenty of time to find out later."

"Will, sometimes I don't know what to make of you."

"How's that?"

"It's just that sometimes you can be as patient as Job and other times you seem to have no tolerance for any kind of delay."

"I don't rightly know what you mean, but that's all right. Can you tell me about this 'blessing'?"

"It is a practice of my church. The men holding the priesthood have the power to act in the name of Heavenly Father."

"Whoa! You mean Bishop Terry and John are 'faith healers'?"

"Not in the way usually known."

"Well, the only faith healers I ever saw was down in Amarillo three years ago at a Chautauqua Tent revival. They were phony as a tin spur."

"No, our people do not use their powers publicly. Almost all blessings, or ministrations, are done privately. They work, Will. I am sure I would have died had I not received the two healing blessings."

"I don't know, ma'am. I like your Bishop and John Terry just fine, but I don't know whether I'm ready to agree that they're messengers of God."

"As much as it bothers me to do so, I am afraid I'm going to have to ask you to have another session with Jess Turner."

"Before I do that, let me ask you a question. Does Bishop Terry actually heal you with one of these 'blessings'?"

"No! Any good and worthy Mormon priesthood bearer can do the same. They are not healing you. They are only the mouthpiece of God from whom comes the healing. If the person blessed has not sufficient faith, either in Heavenly Father, or in the power of the priesthood, the blessing is of no more value than a brief conversation."

"Like you said, the next stormy day, I'll slip over and chat with Jess Turner."

"Are you upset?"

"No, ma'am, I'd say more confused than anything else. Another thing; none of the men from your church, that I've met, act like they have the kind of power you're talking about."

"Humility is an absolute requirement for the power we're talking about."

"Are your priesthood holders always successful in healing?"

"Absolutely not! The blessing is like a prayer. Help is asked for in certain ways that allow God to prompt the brethren what to say. Sometimes it's good news and sometimes not."

"I'd better have that talk with Jess Turner, soon."

"Why don't you go tomorrow? It looks like it'll be a good day for it."

"Yeah, if it keeps up we'll probably have a foot of new snow in the morning."

Chapter 28

I left for Jess Turner's place right after breakfast. I'd gone no more than a mile from the house when something prompted me to swing by the stack-yard, which was what I'd come to call the area of haystacks. I could hear the cattle bawling long before I could see them.

As I rode in among the herd I spotted the first calf. It was lying in the snow with blood all around. At first I thought mountain lion. But, when I looked closer I could see it had been shot. I counted a total of twelve yearling calves that had been shot. I couldn't imagine how anyone could have shot twelve head and we had heard no sound at the ranch. Then it dawned on me; they'd been shot with a pistol. I knew that for some reason the sound of a pistol shot won't echo and carry as far as a rifle shot.

I stopped and sat there among the cattle. I knew the what and I'd guessed the how. But, for the life of me, I couldn't come close to guessing the who or the why.

The whole area was covered with new snow, so I figured any tracks would be gone. However, I did as I had done when I had found the Taylor's tracks. I rode back a ways then began to circle the area where the herd was bunched. I was surprised to find two clear sets of horse tracks in the new snow. I knew that whoever had done this thing was not far ahead of me for it had not quit snowing until after daylight and the hoof prints were sharp and clean.

I had taken to carrying my rifle on my saddle and rolling my gunbelt and pistol and carrying them in my saddlebag. I did not hesitate. I struck out after the tracks which were plain and clear enough to be followed at a long lope. The tracks soon swung around to indicate the riders were either going into the settlement, or close to it. I could have struck out for the settlement, but I decided to follow the tracks as far as I could. I followed them much further than I'd have thought possible. The tracks led right up to the hitching rail in front of John Terry's store. There were two saddled horses tied to the hitch rail. Both carried brands I'd never seen. I stepped off my horse and strapped on my gun belt.

When I walked into the store it was almost empty. There was John and a woman John was helping, and standing over by the stove were the two erstwhile U. S. Marshals. I didn't even slow down. Before they realized it, I was standing within six feet of the two.

"Outside, and right now!" I said.

"What do you want with us, cowboy? We ain't done nothing, and you can't order U.S. Marshals around." This from the big one. The white-haired one had stiffened when he saw me, and stood right still.

"I said outside, and I mean now. I'll not tell you again!"

They looked at one another and turning, started for the front of the store. The white-haired one was in the lead, followed closely by the big one.

As we neared the door, something felt wrong. I was suddenly uneasy and jumpy.

They both went straight out the door, but just as he cleared the door sill, the bigger man stepped quickly aside. When he did, the white-haired one was already turning and fired immediately from his gun which obviously had already been drawn when he was hidden by the bulk of the bigger man.

I felt no pain or constraint so the thought that he had missed crossed my mind as I drew and fired. The sound of my pistol shot, inside the store was deafening. I didn't miss. The man took two or three steps, one to the side and one backwards then seemed just to slowly collapse in a sitting position on the edge of the store's porch. He then slumped forward nearly touching his knees with his forehead.

I turned to the other man who now stood with his hands shoulder high and the palms toward me.

"Don't shoot, cowboy! It weren't my idea. Jake said we'd throw a scare, maybe get you to fight and then leave."

"Who sent you?"

"Jake works or worked, for Tim Johnson, over to Alamosa. Jake hired me ever once in awhile."

"Who's idea was it to kill those calves?"

"I don't rightly know. All I know is Jake came for me out at my cabin and told me we had some livestock to take care of."

Right then I told him to drop his gun belt and after he had done so, I told him to get out of the country and never come back. He headed down the steps then turned to his horse.

"Oh, no you don't," I said. "You just head on out east. You're going to leave here on foot. I'm taking those horses and rigs as part payment for those yearlings you killed."

"But, mister, it's a long two day ride back to Alamosa. I'll most likely freeze to death on foot."

"There's worst ways to die. You want to talk about a couple!"

He looked at me a moment then turned from his horse. He stopped and turned back.

"Is it all right if I take my slicker? It might snow again."

I told him to take what he wanted but to leave the saddle and saddle bags on the horse. He stepped back and untied his slicker and removed two packages from one saddle bag then stepped around to the other side. He reached into the bag to retrieve its contents. I don't know whether it was intuition or the look on his face, but the minute he put his hand in that saddle bag, I started to draw my pistol. I was too late. I felt the sudden shock to my left shoulder that told me, even as I squeezed off my shot, that I'd been hit. I swung back against the door frame and slowly went to my knees. Before I blanked out I could see the big man lying on his side staring at me from eyes wide open, but sightless. I remember thinking that was probably the luckiest shot I'd ever made. The round, black hole in his forehead haunted me for years.

I felt as if someone had thrown me into a sea of fire. I came to and saw John Terry washing my side with the coldest water I'd ever felt. I started to sit up, but the pain made me reconsider.

"Just lie still, Will, you're bad hit," John Terry advised.

I reached over and felt the entry wound, then I asked John where the bullet came out. When he placed his hand on my back just above my belt and towards my side rather than back, I knew I wasn't hit too bad.

I asked John if he would get some strips of cloth and bind up my side. He did, and with his help, I was able to stand. From the location and feel of the wound, I was sure the same ribs the Taylor boy had broken were once again abused.

I asked John to have someone take care of the bodies as I had to get back to the ranch with the two horses.

"Mr. Jackson, I don't know what kind of problem you think you had with those men, but I'll tell you one thing. You will not turn the streets of our settlement into a shooting gallery. This outrageous behavior must stop right here."

"You're not interested in my side of the story?"

"Not really; that you killed these men on the porch of my store is the only side I'll listen to. I'll see these men have a decent burial, and the Bishop and I will be out to see Mrs. Bailey tomorrow."

I said no more, just took a catch rope from Jake's saddle and tied the two animals together then looped the end around my saddle horn. I had to lead my pony to the edge of the porch to mount. After I was aboard, I turned to Terry.

"Mr. Terry, I've never minded dealing with a hard man as long as he's fair. I'll have to say, you're hard."

I turned my little cavalcade and went slowly back to the ranch.

When I finally rode into the door yard. I could not dismount. I sat there like a dummy for several minutes before Seth Blalock came round the corner of the barn in his sleigh.

"Howdy, Will, little cold to just be sitting around, isn't it?"

I grinned and turned my horse toward the water trough, now

frozen over, beside the barn door.

"Seth, am I glad to see you. I'd be much obliged if you'd help me off this horse."

"What's the matter, son, are you hurt?" he asked as he jerked his team to a halt and jumped down.

With Seth's help and using the rim of the water trough as a step, I got to the ground. Standing straight up, I was not too uncomfortable but any side to side movement got my attention right quick.

"What happened, Will?"

"Not much; me and a couple of gents had a little dispute over cattle. They lost, but, not before making my next few nights a little less than restful."

"Man, are you shot? There's blood on your pants leg."

"Yeah, they winged me but I'll be all right. I just need to be in my bed. If you would do me a favor and take care of these horses I'd be obliged."

"You want me to help you to bed?"

"No, I can make it, just take care of the horses."

I turned and went into the barn and on to my room where I collapsed on my bed. I dozed off to awaken to darkness penetrated by a lighted lamp on a small table and Clatilda sitting on the only chair in the room.

When I looked over at her, she had her hands folded in her lap and her head bowed. I gazed at her for several minutes before she looked up. When she saw I was awake, she smiled.

"Where's William?" I asked.

"Annie has him. I knew you'd need care when you awakened."

"You're too sick, yourself, to be sitting out here, out in the cold."

"It's not cold, I lit the fire. And what's more, I'm not sick anymore."

"Well, I'm all right now. You can go back to the house and get some rest."

"Not until I check your wound."

I could see no sense in arguing so I dutifully pulled up my shirt and rolled over on my right side. She had to soak the old bandage to get it off. When she did, I heard her gasp, but she said nothing as she cleaned and re-bandaged both wounds. She then tightly wrapped the bandages and my ribs. When she was done, I rolled on my back.

"Thank you very much, ma'am. Now you'd best go get some rest."

"Before I do that, what happened, Will?"

I told her the whole story including the promised visit by the Terry's.

"Why would those two men kill our cattle, Will? There must be more to this than we know."

"Oh, there's more to it all right. And that 'more' is Tim Johnson. The white-haired one, called Jake, worked for Johnson, according to the one who told you not to move the day they were here."

"Then, we'd better see if the law won't take care of Mr. Johnson."

"You're spitting into the wind, ma'am. He's probably tied to whatever law there is that regulates this part of the country."

"We'll just have to see. But, Will, I've been thinking no one else in this whole area has had any problem with homesteaders. Why us?"

"I've been thinking on that, ma'am. I asked Jess Turner, the last time I saw him and he said he'd checked around after he and the Bishop were out here talking to you about that land pact. He said he could find no evidence that any attempts at homesteading in the entire valley, just on your place. Now, ma'am you go to bed."

"All right, but not until you go back to sleep."

I closed my eyes and got real still. I even managed a snore or two. Even so, it was almost an hour before I heard her, quietly, get up and leave my room and then the barn. I waited until I heard the cabin door close, then I got out of bed and changed my shirt and pants. I then went out to where we kept the saddles and tack. I located the saddles of the men I had killed. There was nothing in the saddle bags of one, obviously the big man's saddle, but I found a wallet in the other set of bags. In that wallet, I found a note. When I read the note I understood why the calves had been shot.

Suddenly, I was very tired and stumbled back to my bed. When I awoke, it was full daylight. I got up and tried to milk but I couldn't handle it. I started to the cabin to see if Annie Blalock was there so that she might milk. As I walked out of the barn, I could see three horses tied by the cabin. I went to the door and knocked. Annie opened the door.

Quietly, she almost whispered, "get in here Will Jackson. They're talking real bad about you."

I asked her if she could milk for me. She said nothing, just stepped around me and headed for the barn.

"Come in, please, Mr. Jackson. It's you we came to talk to."

I walked into the cabin to find Clatilda, John Terry, his son

Joseph and Bishop Terry seated at the table.

"What can I do for you, Bishop?"

"You can try to explain to us why you murdered those two men in front of John's store yesterday."

"I murdered no one. Both of those men fired first."

"John tells me you went into his store and challenged both to go outside."

"He's got that a little wrong. I didn't challenge anyone. I, flat out, told them to get outside. I didn't want John or his customer to get hurt."

"John tells me that these were the men who picked up their weapons at his store, a few months ago. He says they told him they were Marshals."

"John, did you see a badge or any other sort of identification?" Clatilda asked.

"I don't remember badges, but they both had heavy coats on. The badges could have been on their shirt or vest."

"Don't you think it's a little strange, they didn't come right out here and arrest me the minute they got their guns?"

"I did wonder about that."

"Well, let me tell you a little tale about homesteaders, shot cattle and a fellow named Tim Johnson from over at Alamosa."

I then recited the whole tale from when Clatilda and I first noticed the nester's camp smoke through following the two men's tracks in the new snow right up to the hitch rail at John's store. I told them of my brief conversation with the two men, and exactly how the shooting occurred.

"What did you intend to do, Mr. Jackson when you got the two men out in the street?" the Bishop asked.

"Well, Bishop, this may come as a surprise to you, but I was going to disarm them bring them out to your place and ask your advice on what to do. But, know this, I will allow no man to shoot at me. Whether he be marshal, bum or Mormon."

"Well, I'll certainly not have you murdering people in my store, regardless of the reason. If you had not been armed, I'm sure there would have been no shooting," said John.

"Now, sir," said Clatilda standing and walking to a cabinet beside the door to her room, "I believe I have a document here that allows me quite a bit to say about what will and what won't go on in 'your' store. I think it's time we all looked at this incident differently. You both agree that Will shot, only after he was fired upon. I further think you understand he was pursuing my interest as well as the interest of this ranch. It could be this is a situation where a little more understanding is indicated."

"We understand, Sister Bailey," said the Bishop, "but it seems that trouble, gun trouble, has followed this man since the day he came into this valley."

"Yes, Bishop, and that day was the day the Lord chose to take my Jethro. This man was the one who built Jethro's coffin and, in a blinding snow storm, dug my husband's grave. Every bit of trouble he has had, since coming here, has been in the shepherding and protection of a ranch and widow to which he has no claim other than his monthly wages."

"I understand all of that, Sister, but you know we are not thought well of by the other settlers and ranchers in this area. I do not want to see our settlement become unsafe for our women and children."

"I understand, but tell me, Bishop, what would you have Mr. Jackson do?"

"Clatilda, I don't rightly know. I just don't know. I can see yours and Will's side of the picture. But, as you know, I've been through some of the skirmishes we've had with the government and other gentiles. I had hoped we could live and worship quietly in this valley."

"Bishop Terry," I spoke up, "maybe it would be better, all around, if I just pulled up my stakes and rode out of here."

"No . . . Will!" Clatilda said.

"Maybe he's right Clatilda. That would simplify things all around."

"Bishop," I said, "you are not going to find any simple answer to what is facing this ranch. I don't know why, but there is a straight out plan to steal this ranch. I could prove what I say, but I'll only say this, if the takeover is successful, you'll see few quiet days."

"Be that as it may, Mr. Jackson, we lived quietly you came here, and we expect to return to our tranquility. Should problems develop, we will turn to the proper authorities for assistance."

I looked at the man for a moment, then turned and went out of the cabin. As I closed the door, I heard Clatilda begin talking to the Bishop.

I wasted little time in rolling my possibles and saddling my pony. I was so upset that I almost forgot I had several months pay coming. I had, infrequently, drawn money over the past year but the total draw would not much exceed one month's pay. That is discounting the pay Clatilda had given me the first time I'd left.

I actually stopped and studied a moment about not even asking for my pay. But, I figured it was due, and I had earned it.

I knocked on the cabin door to have it opened by Clatilda. As she was opening the door, I heard John Terry say, "Sister Bailey, I see this as a grave mistake."

"Come in, Will." She said stepping back, "I have business with you."

I walked in, not ready for another hassle, but curious.

"Will, I owe you back wages, I believe. As near as I can figure, I believe the amount to be slightly less than four hundred dollars."

"Yes, ma'am, that's about right."

"How would you like to buy into a ranch, Will Jackson?"

"I'd like that just fine, ma'am, but I've got about twenty-six dollars on me and the four hundred you owe me will about make a good down payment on the corral fencing. Nice to talk about, ma'am, but not possible."

"Mr. Jackson, in front of these two witnesses I am offering to sell you fifty-one percent of this ranch for the wages due you. You can keep the twenty-six dollars you have in your pocket!"

I'd been hit in the stomach by a big old drunk miner, one time, up to Leadville. That was just about how I felt then.

"I can't believe you'll make such an offer, ma'am. But before we go any further, I want to know the why and the wherefore."

"It's simple, Will; if, as you say, there is a concerted effort to take over my ranch, it would take me a while to find and hire a ranch foreman and possibly not soon enough would he prove to be as able a protector as I already know you to be. Furthermore, I believe you know more about this plot and its players than I ever will. So, my friend, it comes down, simply, to self survival. Better forty-nine percent of a going ranch than zero percentage of a ranch tied up in unsympathetic courts for who knows how long."

"But, ma'am, why fifty-one percent for me. Why not forty-nine and fifty-one for you. At least, then you would still have control of your own ranch."

"That's just the point, Will. I want that you should be able to act without anyone else's approval or consultation."

I looked straight at her, and she never flinched. She looked right back in that way of hers.

"Bishop," I asked, "how do you feel about this?"

"I am torn between the two sides, Will. I am concerned for the safety of our people and my feelings that somehow this is a good thing Clatilda proposes. I am somewhat against her, basically, giving you controlling interest in her ranch but I honestly can say it seems not to be a bad idea."

"What about me being such a threat to your community?" I asked looking right at John Terry.

"You worry me, Will. It seems where you go, trouble follows."

"I'll not promise you I'll be any different as a ranch owner than I have been as a hired hand. But this I will promise you, John and you also Bishop; I will be just as quick to protect our community as I have been to protect this ranch. And just as violently, if required."

"Our community?" asked the Bishop.

"Yes sir, that is if you'll have me."

"You mean you want to be baptized?" asked John.

"Not yet. I've some more things I want to talk to Jess Turner about."

"Can I help you, Will?" asked the Bishop.

"Not yet. Let me work this out my own way. But the fact I don't carry your brand yet doesn't change the fact I feel I belong to this community."

"But a half hour ago you were ready to leave," John said.

"No, my friend, I wasn't ready to leave, I was all but being kicked out."

The Bishop turned to Clatilda, "Are you straight in your mind. This is what you want?"

"It is the only way that makes any sense. That is, if Will can accept the proposal."

They all turned to see what I had to say . . .

"If I take a portion of the ownership of this ranch, I have two questions and I want an answer from each of you three. First, if it again becomes necessary to protect this ranch in any way, can I expect your help or your condemnation? And, second, can I expect the same help I've received thus far from the men in your church?"

"Let me answer the last question," replied the Bishop, "Of course, as long as you are willing to trade labor, the men of our church will work with you as they have done in the past. Isn't that right, John?"

John looked, first at the Bishop then me.

"Will, I haven't liked the way you run this ranch. That should be clear to you from some of the things I've said. But, in thinking about it, I've realized two things. One is the obvious; if you gave me this whole ranch and all of the livestock on it, I would have no idea where to start or what to do after I got started. The second is I think I may have been too much and too long among ladies shopping for do-dads and drummers selling ribbons. Something else, when I think back on it, it does seem like those two you shot had been hanging around my stove a little longer than is usual."

"Clatilda?" I asked as we all turned to face her.

"Don't give me that 'Clatilda', cowboy. You may run this ranch but I'm not cutting hay for you or anyone else!"

The general soft laughter that followed those remarks set the tone of future relationships between we three men. Relationships I've enjoyed these many years.

Stepping to the stove, Clatilda said, over her shoulder, "I have dried apple pie, and I will make hot cocoa. Who will join me?"

I found that day how difficult it is to harbor a grudge toward anyone with whom you share an apple pie and a pot of cocoa.

Annie didn't come back from the barn until after the three men had gone. She and Clatilda poured more cocoa for the three of us while she and Clatilda argued about whether Clatilda was well enough to fend for herself. It was finally agreed that Annie would come down every two or three days and if Clatilda showed any signs of what Annie called "back-sliding," she, Annie, would start right over with the dawn to dusk routine.

About that time Seth showed up, with the kids, for lunch. All he got was a promise of a meal after they all returned home. Annie left with her family.

Chapter 29

"Now, Mr. Jackson, let's you and I transact our business. I will write up a contract for the sale, and I'll copy the wording from my deed for a quit claim deed from me to you and me."

"Not just yet, ma'am. There are a couple of things we're going to settle before we go any further. As a part owner, I will be able to speak and do for the ranch, right?"

"Absolutely, I only hope you will keep me advised."

"Well, there'll be no problem there, but now, let's talk percentages."

"No, Will, I've made my mind up. You are to have controlling interest."

"Nope, I'll have ten percent and not one whit more. I'll not argue about it or barter my position away for more apple pie. I will become a partner in this ranch, but not the owner-partner, Clatilda, that's final."

"You're serious, aren't you, Will?"

"Yes, ma'am. And I'll not see us arguing over something that can, as easily, be handled one way, as another. Just write out your contract and quit claim deed for ninety and ten instead of fifty-one and forty-nine." She stood and headed for her room. After a few steps, she stopped and came back to my chair. Standing behind me, she placed one hand upon my shoulder. "Will Jackson, I think, in all my life, I've never known a finer man than you."

I don't believe I could have stood, at that moment, if my life depended on it. Funny, but at the same time I felt like running in all directions at once. I could think of nothing to say, but by then it didn't matter for she had quickly turned toward her room again.

She returned with writing materials, the ranch deed and a copy of Jethro's quit claim deed to Jennifer. She said she could copy the wording and property description from Jennifer's deed and put our names in the proper places, and it would be fine.

I sat and watched as she meticulously copied the information and also wrote out the sales agreement between us. It was mid-afternoon before she completed both documents. We both signed and she promised to have John Terry notarize them the next time she went to town. It was only when she mentioned that I should probably ride to Alamosa and file the deed and while there have a copy made that I remembered the note I'd found in Jake's saddle bag.

"Now that the dust has settled, let me show you what everyone almost bought into."

I took the letter from my shirt pocket and read it to her.

"Will, you had this in your pocket, all along, didn't you?"

"Yes ma'am, I got up last night after you left and found it in Jake's saddle bag."

"But, why didn't you mention it to Bishop and John?"

"Wasn't their problem. It's this ranch's concern, and we'll take care of it."

"But how can they support us if they don't have the whole story?"

"Ma'am, in the first place, all this note says is for Jake to kill a few cows and see that I am 'put out of the way.' The cows are dead and putting me out of the way proved to be more than they could handle. The why this was to be done is what troubles me. There has to be a powerful reason for someone to go to all this trouble to get hold of this ranch. What's more, it's clear Johnson knows nothing about you or he'd have known shooting a few head wouldn't drive you from this ranch."

The both sat quietly for a few minutes, Clatilda folding and re-folding the document, and I stared out the window.

"If only we knew why Johnson wants us off this ranch so badly," I mused.

"Maybe he thinks he can control the big valley, somehow, if he gets the ranch."

"I'll bet that's it! These two creeks supply the big valley, too, don't they?"

"Yes but there's the river and one other creek that everyone could depend on, so that's no real threat."

"Well, I just don't know. But, there has to be a reason. Maybe I'll just have me a little chat with Mr. Johnson when I go to Alamosa to file that deed."

"When do you think you'll be well enough to make such a ride?"

"I don't rightly know. Maybe by the first of next week. At any rate, I would like to ride over to Jesse Turner's before Sunday."

Once again I was treated to one of Clatilda's shining smiles. "Go tomorrow, it's too late today," she said.

Chapter 30

Ileft for Turner's the next morning right after breakfast. This time I felt no real compulsion to go by the stack-yard. I went anyway.

I spent most of the day with Jess Turner and his wife, Hester. Sometimes Mrs. Turner was in the room and, more often than not, she was elsewhere in the house. Their home was arguably the most substantial I'd seen in the valley. Jess had hauled logs from the nearby hills and stripped every one. The rock fire place he had built was something to behold. In addition, he had smaller fireplaces in both bedrooms and even in the kitchen. He had laid his house out in such a way that all four fireplaces shared two common chimneys. He'd also done something I thought to be fine and I wished Clatilda had such. Before he built the house, he'd dug his well, cased it, and then built the kitchen over it. He bragged there were no tea kettles of hot water necessary for the pump to work, on even the coldest mornings. He laughingly said the only problem was that if he ever had to pull his pump he'd probably have to take the roof off the kitchen.

This time he didn't wait. Almost as soon as I'd taken off my hat and coat, he asked me if I was ready to be baptized. Again, I told him no, I had more to learn. He jokingly said if I kept postponing baptism to learn more, I'd wind up knowing more than the Bishop and still not be baptized. We hem and hawed around for the better part of an hour then I finally got to the point of my visit.

"Jess, I want you to explain to me this 'blessing' and healing and all these 'priesthood powers'."

I had guessed Mrs. Turner might be listening but when she stuck her head out of the kitchen and asked of Clatilda, I was sure.

"She's much better, ma'am, not as well as she thinks but a lot better than she was."

Mrs. Turner had stepped onto the parlor and she stood there, straight as a stick and looked me right in the eye, much as Clatilda did.

"Will Jackson, my husband thinks very highly of you, but I've got a question."

"Hester!"

"Jess, this needs asking, and you won't. I will. Will, is there anything going on between you and Clatilda Bailey that would keep you from feeling worthy for baptism?"

"Will, I apologize for Hester. Sometimes she speaks as bluntly to others as she does to me."

"No, Jess, that's all right. At least your wife has the courage to ask what others only whisper. No, ma'am, as far as Clatilda is concerned, I am a hired hand. I'm treated somewhat better than most cowboys and I'm occasionally invited to share a piece of homemade pie and a glass of milk. But, no ma'am, there is absolutely nothing going on at the Bailey ranch that you would not be comfortable knowing."

For some strange reason I felt compelled to defend Clatilda. I cited my lowly station, lack of assets and probability I would not soon have any of either. I went on to point out that Clatilda was kind to me but that I suspected that to be in her nature, and I felt she would be as kind to anyone else in my position.

"Will, I'm not questioning Clatilda's motives or her character. I just wanted to know if you were aware of her feelings. You obviously are not."

"Yes, woman, and now, because of your prying, you've created a problem for Will that didn't exist before." Jess scolded.

Hester looked at me for a moment, then turning back into the kitchen, said, over shoulder, "Oh, I don't know, Jess. I may have just answered a couple of questions for Will. Right, Will?"

She was gone before I could answer. Jess started to apologize for her, but I told him not to worry but I did have one question.

"Jess, are your wife and Clatilda related, somehow?"

He sat there a moment, then laughed.

"They do, both, have a direct way about them, don't they? I do wonder if somewhere back down the line they share common ancestry."

We chatted for a few minutes then got back to the subject of my visit. Jess pretty well repeated what Clatilda had said about faith and healing. Then he went further in discussing a father's blessing of his children. He finally made a statement that, to me, made the difference.

"Will, when you're talking about healing, faith and blessings, just remember that there are those who attempt to heal from without; like those people in Amarillo you told me about. The only way healing, based upon faith can occur is from within, and the best any priesthood bearer can do is open that conduit between the Lord and the person in need of such a conduit. The person needing the conduit has two jobs. One is to have faith that such a conduit exists and two, that the brother offering the blessing has the power to open that conduit. Of course, a belief in our Heavenly Father is implied in all instances. But, it's no more complicated or mysterious than that."

He had previously explained the mechanics of the blessing and now I was comfortable with the whole thing. I started to tell him I might accept baptism, but it occurred to me: I knew nothing about the procedure. For the next hour, Jess explained baptism as a covenant as well as the mechanics of the actual baptism. He told me if I was really serious, I should go home and pray about it.

I left the Turners after promising Hester to bring Clatilda the next time. On my way back to the ranch, I swung around the settlement. It was a cold dreary afternoon. Clouds hanging far down the mountain sides promised more snow. I rode along thinking about what all had happened to me this last year and what I'd learned talking to Jess and reading the book. As I was riding across the flats before swinging into our valley, I was thinking hard about baptism and joining the Church. I heard a voice speak just as clear as if there were right beside me. I jerked around in the saddle, but as far as I could see, there was no one in sight. I rode on for another mile or so then I pulled my pony to a stop and thought about what had happened. In the years since, I believe that was the point at which I made two of the most important decisions of my life.

I rode into the door yard just as Clatilda was coming out of her cabin with a water pail. She invited me in for supper after I'd stabled my horse and milked. These chores took longer than usual because my thoughts were so intense that they tended to slow me down.

When I went into the cabin, Clatilda was just dishing up dinner.

"Did you learn anything more?" she asked as I sat to the table.

"Yes, I think I learned a lot. In fact, maybe some more than I'd counted on."

"What do you mean?"

"Clatilda, if I ask you something will you try not to be upset?"

She looked long at me then down at her plate. "Go ahead, I'll be all right."

I didn't immediately understand her response.

"Clatilda, Hester Turner said something to me that I must know if it's true. I guess the only way to really know is to outright ask. Clatilda, will you marry me?"

"Yes."

"That's all, just yes?"

"Yes, Will."

"Don't you want to talk about it? Maybe, like how I'm going to support you or any of those things women are supposed to worry about? You've only known me just over a year; you don't really know anything about me."

"Are you trying to talk me out of this, or yourself?"

"No, I am not trying to talk you out of anything. It's just that your answer was so fast out, and definite."

"Would you be happier if I simpered and whined and took two days to give you an answer? You asked me if I'd marry you, and I said I would. What more do you want to hear?"

"Oh, I don't know. I expect, in all honesty, I thought you'd probably say no."

"Why should I do that?"

"I've nothing to offer. Oh, you gave me ten percent of this ranch and I have about four hundred dollars owed and earned, but when you come right down to it, I have no more than when I rode down off that mountain to kill a bear."

"Will, are you trying to back out of your proposal?"

"No, not at all. I guess I just can't believe anyone like you would ever think enough of me to agree to marriage."

"Will, I offered you marriage, once before. It was a very embarrassing thing to do. You thought it to be strictly a business proposition, then. I'll tell you it wasn't then, nor is it now."

"Then, I'd better move into the settlement until after we are married."

"Why in the world would you do that?"

"Well, I don't think it would be right for us to continue living as we are, what with our going to get married, and all."

She smiled that sweet, bright smile of hers. "Will Jackson, there's no need for that. As long as we do not allow anything improper to happen, who is to be concerned? And, cowboy, there will be no impropriety, not at least until you put that gold ring on my finger, and I don't care for long engagements."

She got up from the table and came around to my side and kissed me on the cheek, then returned to her chair.

"What have you decided about joining the Church?" she asked.

"Does it matter, as far as our getting married is concerned?"

"Well, it's sort of like having a piece of home made pie. It's always better with a little cream on top. Your joining the Church would be the cream on top."

I told her about the experience I'd had on the way home, hearing that voice, and all. She looked at me for a moment with the strangest look on her face, I was afraid I'd done something wrong.

"Will, do you know, I've been a member of this church for almost seven years and never had such an experience? I've received, what I thought, were answers to my prayers but I've never been directly spoken to, as you were today."

"What do you think it meant?"

"Have you thought about it much?"

"Yeah, quite a bit, but when I do, I come back to the same point. Why me?"

"Why not? You said you were thinking about the Church and me. Will, oft times such thoughts become prayers. Are you sure you didn't just get an answer to your prayers?"

"I've thought about that, some. But, why me?"

"Why not? Will, you are a good man. Why haven't you the right to expect to have your prayers answered?"

We sat there at the table for several minutes, each lost in our thoughts. Clatilda got up to clear the dishes.

"Tell me, again, what the voice said?" she asked.

"It was just as clear as what you're saying right now. It said,

'Why do you wait for me? I wait for you."

"It doesn't get more clear than that."

"I know and I guess that's what scares me. How long would it take for me to be baptized?"

"Why don't we leave right after breakfast tomorrow and go in and talk to the Bishop?"

"All right, but then we'd have to get back so I can get some work done. I've still got a ranch to run."

Chapter 31

Mid-morning, the next day, found us in the Bishop's home, waiting in his parlor while one of his boys' fetched him from the barn.

We left right after noon after joining the Bishop and his wife at their noonday meal. We had a date for my baptism and a date for our marriage. Just that easily, I had placed myself in two positions I had never expected to occupy. We drove through the settlement and a mile or so beyond before either of us had much to say. Finally, Clatilda broke the silence.

"Will, do you regret what commitments you've made in the past twenty four hours?"

"Absolutely not! Why would you ask such a question?"

"You've been so very quiet and moody this morning, I just wondered."

"Well, ma'am, if you'll just stop and consider the changes in my life in those same twenty-four hours, I think I've got a right to be a little quiet."

"All right, cowboy, but just wait until I get you home! I've got a big chocolate cake in the warming oven and milk chilling on the window sill. We'll have us a party."

The next two weeks went by in a blur. I asked permission and had Jess Turner baptize and confirm me. After the confirmation Hester Turner came over to Clatilda and me.

"You know, Clatilda, I didn't think this man was ever going to get enough gumption to take one important step, let alone two. But, I think the Lord and I were working together."

"You and a dollop of cream," I said.

Hester looked at me as if I had taken leave of my senses.

"Oh, don't mind him, Sister Turner, that's just a little joke between Will and me."

"Well, you're marrying a hard man, Clatilda. Just love him and keep him close to home."

"I intend doing just that. But rather than 'keeping' I thought to make him want to stay close."

Hester smiled, and Jess Turner stood with his hand on my shoulder.

Clatilda and I were married the following Friday after my baptism. I expected it to be a short, simple, ceremony and then we'd go home. There must have been two hundred people at the wedding and such a supper afterwards! We didn't leave the church until after nine.

On William's birthday, we had quite a celebration. Clatilda invited the Blalock children, and she decorated the cabin specially.

During the party I was talking to Seth about his homesteading attempt. At first he thought I was just ragging him. But, when he saw I was serious, he told me all I wanted to know. Seth and Annie had not selected the land, on our ranch, to homestead. He had been sought out by Tim Johnson. He and Annie were on their way to New Mexico territory and had no intent to stop short of land available for homestead around Tucumcari. He said Johnson came to their camp and started telling them about this wonderful area north west of Alamosa. Plentiful water, timber for their house and neighbors; some Mormon, some not.

Seth said Johnson had agreed to give them a map and file their claim for a finder's fee of a dollar an acre. He and Annie had discussed the issue and decided, with only a few misgivings to accept Johnson's offer.

"Tell me, Seth," I asked, "did Johnson say anything else about the land or the creek?"

"Yeah, he said if I didn't like the set-up to go ahead and prove up, and he'd come over and maybe buy me out."

"Did he say why?"

"No, just that he often bought homesteads to bring more settlers into the country, who would prefer property already 'proved-up'."

After everyone had left, Clatilda and I sat at the table, eating our small piece of the birthday cake while William took a much needed nap.

"What do you want me to do about the ranch, Will?" Clatilda asked.

"I don't know of anything we have to 'do', besides work it, and hopefully, make it pay."

"What I am asking is: do you want to change the deed and put it in your name?"

"You know, Clatilda, I've been giving that a lot of thought, and I've decided what I want you to do."

She looked at me strangely and, rather quietly, asked what I had in mind.

"I want you to make out a quit claim deed to William and another paper that I'm to run the ranch until William is old enough to run it himself, say eighteen or nineteen. Then if anything happens to you, he'll be taken care of and you'll not have to worry."

"But, Will, what about you?"

"I've been thinking about that, too. I figure two or three years from now, we ought to be able to sell off a nice crop of steers. If we do, I think I'm going to see if you won't give me a ten-dollar raise."

Once again, I was favored with one of her sweet smiles. She stood and began clearing the table.

"Well, cowboy, don't expect a raise anytime soon; not with my wood box practically empty."

Chapter 32

The next day was Christmas, and I've never had such a day. With Hester Turner and John Terry helping I was able to order a new cloth coat with a fur collar and a matching fur hat for Clatilda. I don't know which made me prouder; being able to give her the gift, or how pleased she was with it.

Under the tree I found a good sweater and several pairs of socks Clatilda had knitted, unbeknownst to me. I was right pleased. After the presents were all opened, Clatilda went back into the store room and emerged with a long slender package. She handed it to me without comment. I opened it to find a brand-new Winchester.

"I noticed how your rifle was pretty badly beat up," she said, as I turned the rifle round and round, "it seemed a nice thing for you to have."

"I don't know how to ever thank you. But, I would not have

expected such a thing from you. Where in the world did you get the money for such a gift?"

"Are you forgetting we own part of a general store?"

"Yes, in fact, I had. Sometimes I forget that I married a lady of property."

"Well, sir, you are also a person of property. Last week, John and I drew up a new agreement placing your name, along with mine, on the store ownership."

I didn't know what to say. I think I was more embarrassed than anything else.

"Don't you want to know how much of the store you own?"

"No, I don't. And, what's more, I want you never to tell me, regardless of whose name may appear on what paper, that is always to be yours and yours alone. It will please me to see you have the independence that comes from such ownership."

She stood, looking at me for a moment while one large tear, from each eye, coursed down her cheek.

"What's wrong, what have I done?"

She quickly wiped the tears from her cheeks and turning to the stove opened the oven to check the turkey Jess Turner had given us.

When she straightened up, she turned to face me. "No cowboy, you have done nothing wrong. But, you have given me a finer gift than I ever thought to receive."

Chapter 33

It snowed from the day after Christmas into the end of January. It would snow for a while, then clear up and turn deadly cold. Then, almost in an instant, warm a little and start snowing again. Seth and I were kept busy feeding the cattle. We'd decided to move the whole herd on his land to better care for them in the snow. Those five weeks were some of the worst I'd ever put in.

It cleared the last week in January and we hoped we were out of the worst. We were wrong. On the fourth of February, it snowed over a foot in less than three hours. It then cleared. Then the bottom fell out of the thermometer. I don't really know how cold it got, but I know if it hadn't been for the creek we'd have lost the whole herd. As it was, Seth and I spent half of every day chopping the ice so the cattle could drink. It was the third week in February when I went out one morning to check the herd and saw Seth coming toward me with a rifle across his saddle.

"Going bear hunting, Seth?"

"You're not too far off," he responded, "I've got to go hunt us up some meat. We've been out for two days, now, and in this weather, a body needs what only meat can satisfy."

I thought for a moment then shook out my rope. "Seth, we've got a couple of older cows I'd intended to cull anyway. Give me a hand, and we'll take one up to my barn and butcher it. You can take half and we'll keep the other."

"You sure?"

"Sure as the sun coming up in the east. Come on let's get the ice chopped out then we'll get to the barn. It's got to be warmer than it is out here."

Seth proved to be a much better hand at butchering than I and by late afternoon we had our half hung, and ready and he was headed home with his half.

The next time I saw Annie, she hugged me and thanked me for the meat. I told her she should hug Seth as he'd done the work that required skill.

"Oh," she said, "I did, several times!"

The winter finally broke in mid-March. It seemed one day it was dark and freezing and the next the sun actually gave some warmth. After that, it was a downhill ride right into early summer.

One day Clatilda and Annie had taken the children and driven to the settlement for supplies. I had been working the cattle preparing for branding when Daniel Blalock came riding toward me on Clatilda's bay horse. He said I was to get home right away. He said Clatilda had told him to tell me, no one was hurt or anything like that, but I'd better hurry, she wanted to talk to me.

By the time I'd reached the house, Annie, Clatilda and all the kids were inside.

When I walked in, Clatilda was at the table. She stood and stepped toward me.

"Will, we have more trouble with homesteaders."

"How do you know?"

"There were four wagons, with families, at the store. John said they were spending money like they had lots of it. He said they had bought everything from tools to flour. He said he'd never seen farmers with so much cash. I find it hard to believe. Their wagons and harness all looked practically new. But, the men, women and children were generally dirty and unkempt. The two don't seem to fit."

"How do you know they will cause us trouble?"

"Because, we waited at the store until they left then we followed them to where our west creek goes around that tall bluff. They turned up the creek, and we came on home on the trail."

"If they came around that bluff, it's only a couple of miles until they're on our place."

"That's what I thought so we watched, as well as we could. I'm sure they are north of the stack yard."

"Are you sure they are homesteaders? What did you think, Annie? Are they homesteaders or travelers?"

"I'll answer that, Will," Clatilda interrupted, "if Seth and Annie are homesteaders, these people are not. That would be like comparing a silk purse to a sow's ear."

Annie gave her a look that was pure love. "No, Will, I don't know what they are, but they're like no settlers I've ever seen. There are just too many things about them that don't fit. In the first place, I've not seen any farmer that had the loose money they were spending. Why, one of the women even bought one of those sewing machines. I should be so lucky!"

"All right, you ladies go on about your business. Daniel can help you unload. I'll take a ride down there."

"If you'll wait a minute, Will, I'll send Daniel after Seth. He'll go with you."

I looked at her a moment, then chuckled.

"What's so funny, Will Jackson?" Annie demanded.

"I will not ask Seth go on this errand with me. He'd never let me live it down!"

Annie stood quietly for a moment then she too chuckled. "Aye, and that would be a bit ironic, wouldn't it?"

I saddled my pony then went into the cabin to get my new Winchester. Clatilda came out of the store room as I was standing beside the table loading my rifle.

"Will, please be careful. The men in this group appear not to be like Seth Blalock. I'd trust them, not at all."

The ride along the creek was pleasant in the warm afternoon. I saw several fish breaking the water, feeding on the May flies. It would have been nice to have spent a lazy hour or so catching our supper, but now I was a man of property and had to protect that same property.

Sure, I thought and what did you do the same thing for last year. For your property or for forty a month and board. That's what this is really all about; married to it or paid by it, you just ride for the brand.

I turned away from the stream and rode another mile before I came to the first camp. It was a shambles. They could not have been there for much more than two hours, but their possessions were scattered in a circle around the wagon. Their horses were still hitched to the wagon, but someone had placed good sized rocks on either side of all four wheels. I sat for a moment looking at the mess.

A brand-new plow had either been thrown or dropped from the wagon and now lay on the ground with one handle broken completely off. A tall angular man stepped around the wagon and walked toward me.

"You one of them Mormons that ain't going to let us homestead here?" was his greeting.

I sat for a minute then shifted my weight, slightly. "Mister, I guess you got that just right."

"Well, Mr. Mormon, we ain't moving. We don't have to. If you give us any trouble, they'll get the army down on you like bees on honey."

"Who are they, my friend?"

"Why the law in Alamosa, that's who!"

"The law wouldn't be named Johnson, would it?"

"Mr. Johnson said you'd come. He said we weren't to leave. He and his people would be here in two weeks and then they would straighten you out."

"Mister, I don't know who you are. I don't know who the rest of your trashy party is, either. But, I'm telling you, once; get out of this valley by this time tomorrow or by dark tomorrow night you'll walk out with nothing but the clothes on your back."

I turned, before he could answer, and rode back to the ranch. I told Clatilda I was going in to talk with Bishop Terry and John.

I found John in his store and, he and I went out to the Bishop's place.

I told them both of the situation, and John repeated what Clatilda had said about the people spending so much money. John said it was the best day he'd had, since opening the store.

"Now, Bishop, you and John got upset the last time I protected the Bailey ranch. Maybe, because I was just a hired hand, I don't know. But things have changed. I will not tolerate these squatters any more than I would the last bunch. I am satisfied these people have been paid to come here. Try as I have, I cannot figure why. But that matters not. I intend to see them off the J-B by dark tomorrow evening."

"Your attitude seems altogether reasonable, Will," said the Bishop. "Let's see if we can't convince these folks they made a mistake. John and some of the brethren and I will be at your place right after noon tomorrow. We'll go from there."

"I did not come for your help, Bishop. I came only for your advice and to tell you, beforehand, of my intent."

"You can't know how your coming at all, pleases me. My advice is wait for us. We'll be there right after noon to support you, brother."

I rode home that clear mountain evening with a feeling I thought I'd lost in my childhood. For too many years, I'd lived with no more family than my horse and saddle. I could not get used to the feeling that I now had a family. An awful big family, but family nevertheless. I somehow felt more anchored and more belonging than I ever had.

When I got home Clatilda was anxious to know what had

happened. I told her of the arrangement and when I'd finished, all she said was, "that's as it should be." With that, she turned to the stove to dish up my supper.

Chapter 34

I spent the morning, that next day, pushing the herd back into Seth's upper pasture. He was already preparing the lower half of his ground for planting, but the upper pasture would carry the herd for a week or so. I didn't want to worry about them in the area south, near the squatter's camps.

I had just finished lunch and stepped out of the cabin to go turn Clatilda's goats into another pasture when I looked south to see a large group of men come riding up the trail, right into the door yard. Counting Bishop Terry, John and his son, there must have been twenty-five or more. They were armed with everything from old ball and cap pistols to late model Winchesters and scatter-guns.

"Bishop, you look like an army, going to war," I said, by way of greeting.

"I hope not Brother Jackson, wars are for dying. Better we should enforce peace upon those who might not be so inclined."

I quickly glanced at him. He was as serious as a broken leg.

"Well, let me get my rifle, and let's get it over!"

I went in and told Clatilda while I was loading my Winchester.

"You will be careful, please," she said. "I'll have supper ready when you return."

When we rode out I felt like some general leading his troops to a peace treaty meeting. Except that everyone was carrying a loaded firearm.

I had asked the Bishop, before we left if all these men knew the whole situation. He said he'd explained it all to them. I commented that he must have been up all night, to tell my tale to so many. He said, no, he'd just put out the word that I had trouble and needed help. He said he'd asked for twenty-five to come. When they showed up at John's store that morning, he'd explained to all twenty-five at once.

"You mean two dozen men showed up because I am in trouble."

"No."

"But you said . . . ," I started to say. "I said twenty-five men, not twenty-four."

By that time I was mounted. He just nodded his head and suggested we might go then.

As we rode down the valley, I got to thinking. If I got this kind of support all the time, I was in real danger of getting fat and lazy.

When we got within a half mile of the camp, I pulled up and told all the men what I'd worked out in my mind that morning. I was going to try to find out why these people were there and exactly the terms under which they had been sent. All agreed there had to be a reason for the squatters consistently trying to settle on deeded land. With such single mindedness we rode into the northern-most camp.

"Well, I see you brought your army with you!" stated the man I'd previously talked to, stepping from behind the wagon.

If possible, the area was even more littered than it previously had been.

"Mister, my name is Will Jackson. My wife and I own the land you're squatting on. Our deed is on file in Alamosa. What made you think this land was open to homesteading?"

"Mr. Johnson said you'd say something like that, but to pay you no never mind. He said if you tried anything, the courts would take care of you!"

"Let me ask you something, friend; why do you have all new equipment?"

"That ain't none of your business!"

"Before we go any further, let's get a couple of things clear. You're not homesteading or squatting here. Secondly, the only reason you're not on the road out of here or standing here watching everything you own burn to the ground is I want some information. Now, tell me, where did you get your equipment, and who paid you to come here?"

"You mess around with us, and I'll have the army on you."

"All right, friend, you can believe in that 'army' stuff that Johnson told you, but, now, let me tell you how it's going to be."

I gigged my pony right up in front of him to the point he took a step backward.

"You've got about ten seconds to start answering my questions, then I'm going to start shooting. I'll start with that Jersey cow."

"Mister, you'd better leave me alone, I've a woman and kids back there."

"Half your time's gone, squatter," I said as I cocked my rifle.

"You wouldn't be so tough if you didn't have all those folks to back you up," he whined.

"You bet your life, squatter, and there's not a man back there but what is twice as tough as me." I raised my rifle and aimed at the cow.

"Don't shoot, mister. That's the only thing that really belongs to us! Jason you tell this man what he wants to know or I will." This from a woman stepping out from behind the wagon.

"What is it you want to know, then?" the man asked.

"You heard me, before. Who sent you here, and what was the money agreement?"

"Mr. Tim Johnson, of Alamosa paid me one hundred dollars, cash money to homestead this land. Plus that he gave me a new wagon, and team and money for farming equipment."

"Now, what's Johnson supposed to get from you?"

"Nothing worthwhile. He just made me sign a paper giving him mineral rights on my homestead."

"Didn't he tell you I was liable to run you off?"

"Yeah, but he said he'd sent two families out here over a year ago and you only run off one. So, he said if four of us came, at least two would probably stay. We all figured to be one of those two."

"Well, Jason, whatever your name is, you are not going to be one of those two. I'm going on down the creek but five of these men are going to stay here while you load up. Anything you don't have loaded by an hour before sundown, they'll burn or destroy."

As I started to turn, he took a step towards my horse. I spun my pony around and pointed my rifle right at his middle.

"Jason, a piece of advice; don't ever make a sudden move at a fellow who's holding a rifle on you."

"I just wanted to ask you if we could take a couple of days. We're all settled in. It might take a while to reload."

I looked around at the pile of trash that had once been a pleasant meadow and creek bank.

"Friend, I'll be back about dark. If you are still here, I'll burn everything you have including all of your stock."

I turned and rode over beside Bishop Terry.

"Bishop, would you ask five of your men to stay here until they leave."

"I have already named five you wanted to stay. What instructions would you have me give them?"

"Look tough but don't harm anything or anyone. I think these folks will leave soon."

He looked at me, strangely, then rode over to a small group of men, spoke to them briefly, then rejoined me as we headed south to the next camp.

"Brother Jackson," Bishop asked, "you weren't really going to shoot that Jersey, were you?"

"Bishop Terry, if I'd have shot that milk cow, Clatilda would have chopped me up in little-bitty pieces and fed me to her goats!"

"I don't know why, but I thought that to be the case. Oh, the women, God bless them; they do keep us on the straight and narrow, don't they?"

"Bishop, there are people in this world that would laugh right in your face if you told them I had joined your church, Clatilda's influence, notwithstanding."

In the second and third camps the squatters had less back bone than Jason. All I had to do was ask and they told me everything. Their stories mirrored Jason's.

When we rode into the fourth camp I had a funny feeling. I told the Bishop to stay back about a hundred feet while I rode into the camp.

There were two men in the camp and no women or children; that I could see.

"You the big bad rancher that's going to run us off?" said one stepping away from the wagon.

I glanced around the camp. They had unpacked nothing, only a coffee pot sitting on a rock beside their campfire. Even the mules were staked close to the wagon.

"No, I just came to warn you."

"Warn all you want, mister, you ain't running us off our homestead."

"Suit yourself. But you see those men out there?"

"You're still short of enough men to make us leave. Me and my partner have fought twice that many Indians, all to once, and we've still got our hair!"

"You don't understand, sir. Those fellows back there are Company A of the Zion Militia. You have chosen to squat right on their target range. Twice a week they ride out here from town and set up over east in that bunch of trees and use the bank, across the creek behind you, as targets. If you chose to stay here, things could get a little hairy. But, you do what you've a mind to." I turned then and rode back to the men. I quickly instructed them to get behind the biggest pine tree they could find. When they were all under cover, the Bishop, John Terry and I went among them with instructions. We told them to begin firing at will. Just be sure to fire very high or very wide.

When we were all set, I opened the ball. I didn't shoot high or wide. My first shot busted a dirt clod right in front of the man I'd talked to. He jumped like a startled quail. His partner made one quick dive and was under the wagon. The one I'd spoken to began waving his arms and yelling. I sent the word down the line for the men to stop shooting. When all had quieted down the man yelled for me to come out and talk. He was less than seventy-five feet from the rock behind which I knelt.

"Talk if you want. I can hear you!" I yelled.

"Mister, you're getting yourself in trouble with the army. I'll have them out here so quick you won't know what hit you!"

"Then, I guess there's no reason to save you. It will be good practice for the militia to shoot you and your partner. You want me to turn them loose?"

His partner must have said something to him for he turned to the wagon and after a few moments turned back toward us and began waving his arms over his head, again yelling for "the rancher."

"What now?" I shouted.

"We're leaving, just don't do no more shooting."

"That's fine. Now I want both of you to lay your handguns and rifles there by the wagon tongue and go over there by those two big cedars. Stand right up against the trunk and reach as high up as you can."

They did as told and we all rode out together, right up beside the wagon.

"Bishop," I said, "have four of your folks check those two for hideout guns, and the rest unload and reload the wagon. I do not want a single weapon, firearm or knife left in this camp." In all, we found three pistols, two rifles plus the two pistols and two rifles thrown down by the would-be homesteaders.

When we'd gathered up this small arsenal, I had the men back off away from the wagon. I rode over beside the cedars and pulled up in front of the two.

"You have fifteen minutes to harness and hitch your team, five more minutes to be on the road and one hour to be east of the settlement."

"But, mister," spoke up the one who'd hidden under the wagon, "its gotta be better than five miles to that settlement!"

"All right, if you're going to whine about it, you have one hour and ten minutes from right now to be east of the settlement. Would you like to try for an hour, flat?"

They said not another word. It took only ten minutes for them to be turning their team on the trail south.

Bishop and John Terry rode up beside me. Bishop suggested I return to the ranch as Clatilda had surely heard all the shooting. He said he and the other men would escort these gentlemen out of the country. I told them I'd ride by the other three camps and make sure they were also moving out.

All three of the other camps were deserted when I rode through. I was decked out like an army. All the firearms from the southern camp were draped around me and my saddle. I was sort of glad I didn't see anyone.

I found it interesting that Jason's camp was still a mess with tools, bedding and other junk still strewn around. I would tell Seth about it. He could probably use some of the tools, especially the brand new turning plow with the broken handle.

As I rode back to the ranch, I wondered how Mr. Johnson would take this recent turn of events. It came to me why Johnson wanted homesteads on that creek and particularly 'the mineral rights' on those homesteads. I resolved to talk to Clatilda tonight and Seth tomorrow. I didn't have to talk to Seth.

Clatilda met me in the door yard when I rode in. She was, as Bishop Terry suggested, worried about the gunfire she'd heard. I told her about what we'd done and she laughed, saying I'd either become too much of a Mormon or too little. She said she'd have to think on it to decide.

She came into the barn with me while I stabled my horse and put the many guns away. When she asked me what I was ever to do with so many firearms, I told her of how some of the men from the Church carried really old pieces and that I was going to ask the Bishop to give them out according to need.

After we'd finished supper that evening, I told Clatilda about the mineral rights thing Johnson had wanted from the homesteaders.

"I don't know for sure, but I think there may be gold in that creek. Do you think that might be possible?"

"Of course it is!"

"Well, I don't know if I'm that positive, but I intend to check it out."

"There's no need. The gold is there. Jethro worked it before he died."

"You mean you've known all along there was gold in that stream? Why didn't you tell me?"

"Frankly, Will, I didn't think anyone else knew. I always thought of it as a little nest egg. How do you think Jethro got the money he had plus the partnership in John Terry's store?"

"I thought you said he had some rich relative who died."

"Yes, but Jethro's inheritance covered only a portion of the cost of this ranch. Had Jethro not found the gold the first night we arrived and camped along the creek, we'd probably have one of the smaller farms in the big valley or a little ranch up here."

I thought on that for a few minutes before I spoke again. "Do you suppose I could know where this gold is?"

Clatilda sat and looked at me long enough that I felt a rising of anger and bewilderment.

Finally she spoke. "Will, I have done you a terrible injustice, and I am sorry. In the back of my mind was the fact of the gold, but foremost I wanted not to have this area overrun by people with gold fever. I was wrong in not counseling with you. We will go down in the morning first thing, and I'll show you where the gold is."

"That's all right, you don't have to apologize to me. We'll go down in the morning but just to ride by the location. We'll not stop, then we'll come back and talk it over."

When we rode past the next morning, there was little to distinguish the site where Jethro had taken the gold except for a house-sized, granite boulder on the other side of the creek.

When we returned to the cabin, Clatilda asked me if I intended to work the gold. I told her no, that I rather liked the idea of having a nest egg. I told her that for awhile the previous evening, I'd thought seriously of taking out all the gold I could.

"But, ma'am, that really wouldn't make any sense. You married me to get out of having to pay me my back wages. No telling what you'd do to keep me from becoming a gold baron."

"Will Jackson, I don't know whether to break your head with a rolling pin or shock you even more."

"I think the rolling pin would be all the 'shock' I could take."

"You think so? Well cowboy, hang on to your hat! You're going to be a father!"

I sat there for a moment with thoughts going through my mind that I'd never figured to have. As numb as my mind seemed to be, I still had bundles of thoughts and fears of my future.

"Clatilda, are you sure, what if something happens to you? What if you get sick?"

"What if you be quiet, Will. I'm strong and healthy. There is no reason we cannot have a family."

The longer I sat there, the more confused I became. Then, as if curtains opened, my future activities became crystal clear to me.

"Clatilda, I will be leaving for Alamosa at first light tomorrow. I'll go across the mountain. That should save me at least half a day, I've got to settle this thing with Johnson. I'll not have this hanging over you, William and the baby."

"I knew this time would come, and you know, Will, for some reason I'm not particularly worried."

Chapter 35

Daylight found me far up the mountains east of the ranch. I was surprised how easy the climb had been. When the sun started sifting through the big pines it seemed the temperature dropped twenty degrees. After fifteen or twenty minutes it started to warm again. When I started down the eastern side of the mountains it warmed considerably.

I had been right about saving time. I rode into Alamosa a little after midnight. I was able to see the small twinkling lights go out one by one for better than an hour before I rode up to a livery stable. The hostler was sitting on a bale of hay near two double stalls. Probably the warmest place in the barn. I shook him awake and had him stable my horse. With his direction, I walked down the street to a small hotel.

I had breakfast, that next morning, at a café just across the street from the hotel. I was there a little early, as there was only one other person there when I entered. I waited until he left, then asked the lady waiting the counter if she knew a Tim Johnson.

"Si, Senor, I have reason to know that coyotero!"

"Do you know where I might find him?"

"Si, he has his office over the saddle makers. Be careful, when you deal with that one Senor."

"How's that, ma'am?"

"He is not honest. He is a lawyer, but he's not honest."

This, I thought, may not be quite as easy as I'd hoped.

I left the café as people were beginning to stir around the village. I had an idea and walked on down the street looking for an assayer. I found one on a side street and as I walked up the assayer was just unlocking the door.

"Little early, ain't you cowboy?" he said as I stopped beside him.

"Yeah, I thought I'd stop by with a question or two of the only man in town likely to have the answers."

"Well, come on in. It will likely take me but a minute or so to tell you all I know."

After he had lit the lamps, we talked for a little about the different ores he had displayed in a glass case. I told him I had prospected up around Leadville a couple of years back, but went bust. I told him I had gone back to Texas and worked me up a road stake and was ready to go back to prospecting. I asked him if he could point me in a likely direction.

"Cowboy, if you went busted prospecting in that Leadville country, you can't be much of a prospector. Why I was reading the other day where some old boy took over a hundred thousand dollars worth of wire gold out of one small granite shelf."

"Yeah, but let me tell you something, friend. They don't write in the newspapers about the busted prospectors willing to do almost anything for stage fare to Tincup or Denver City."

"Well, I expect that may be a fact. As far as gold around this country. If I was you, I'd head up in the Sangre De Cristo country. I've heard of some good strikes in those mountains."

"Go into the high country, this time of year?"

"You asked, cowboy. It don't make me no never mind if you go prospecting out in the middle of the Gulf of Mexico. You asked where I thought there might be gold, I told you!"

"I didn't mean anything. Might you know of anything a little flatter. I'm from down in the Panhandle country. I was kind of hoping to work some of the creeks around here."

"Well, from time to time, I've had fellows bring in a little dust and even two or three small nuggets they said they'd gotten around here. But, most of the big buys I've made have been from the Sangre De Cristos."

"You've bought big strikes from that country?"

"Yeah, some pretty good sized ones. From time to time, as much as fifty or sixty thousand. Even had one, once, for eighty-two thousand."

"Where'd that one come from?"

"That one, I don't rightly know. Young fellow came in here in a team and wagon. He brought a handful in. Can you believe that?" He walked through that door with a handful of raw gold. Oh, there was a little mica mixed in, but mostly it was all the real stuff. You know what he had the rest of it in? Milk cans! Three milk cans. I'd never seen anything like it in my twenty-five years in this business. When I asked him where it had come from. He jerked his thumb northeast toward the Sangre De Cristos.

"Where do you think his gold came from?"

"You know, I've thought about that, some. I don't believe it came from the high country. I've seen gold from all over the mountains, but none like this. This stuff had been washed quite some distance then probably lodged in the bank of some creek."

"Where do you think a fellow might start looking for that gold?"

"I wouldn't have any idea. One thing about that fellow, most of the men who come in here tend to swear some. That fellow never said a cuss word the whole time he was in here. Even when he spilled some out of one of the milk cans. He just got down and swept it up with his bandanna. Must have been three or four hundred dollars on that floor and you'd have thought he was picking up a dime. Never even a cross word let alone a cuss word."

"Well, I guess I'd better find me some place where they don't swear much!" I said. And he, wryly, replied that it might take a while to find.

I thanked him and started out the door when he called me back.

"You know, cowboy, you might have just hit the nail on the head."

"How's that?"

"I'd not put the two together, but we have a lawyer here in town that seems to be digging up an army of homesteaders to settle out west of here. And, he's filing mineral rights on all of their homesteads. You know where he's sending them to homestead?"

"No idea. Is it important?"

"Yeah, because he's sending them in among the only people I know of here about's that don't do any cussing, to speak of."

"Oh, where are these folks?"

"There's a bunch of them Mormons settled over west of here, about a two-day ride. I've heard they're in a couple of valleys over there. One big one and a smaller one that fingers off to the south. Lawyer Johnson is trying to get those folks to homestead that upper valley. At least that's where he's filing on mineral rights."

"You suppose there's a map somewhere I could locate this valley a little closer than 'west of here'?"

"I'll go you one better, cowboy! Come on, you come with me. We'll go over to the courthouse, and we'll find out together. That Johnson fellow's always been a little too slick for my taste."

We went to the courthouse where Mr. McAvery, the assayer, seemed to know everyone by their first name. They generally allowed him free run of the big record books. He wasted no time noting filing numbers and other information, He was reading through one book when he slapped his hand on the table.

"I've gotcha now, you four flusher!"

"Who you got?"

"I've got that Tim Johnson. That crook has filed for mineral rights on deeded property that he is trying to get homesteaded. Why that no good scoundrel has gotten things so fouled up. He could keep this running around the courts for years."

"You mean this gold may be on someone's private land?"

"Here's the deed, plain and clear. There's the legal description, and here's the descriptions from the mineral rights assignments Johnson has filed."

"Do you have a sheriff in this place?" I asked.

"Yeah, cowboy, we've got us a real good sheriff, but what do you want with him?"

"Could I trouble you to go with me for a while longer?"

He looked at me a long moment, then slammed the book shut, returning it to the shelves.

"Yeah, cowboy, I think I will. I've got me a strange feeling this might turn out to be fun."

We went down a long hallway to the sheriff's office which was also there in the courthouse. I noticed from the sign on the door, the sheriff's name was James Nava. Mr. McAvery chuckled at the sign.

"His real name is Jamie, pronounced 'Hymie' but as a concession to the Anglos who voted him in and a real crook out, he officially goes by James. But, to us, his old friends, he'll always be Jamie."

We walked into a two-office setup that was clean to the point of appearing barren. There were no spittoons, no paper trash, no stale odors just the smell of gun oil and fresh scrubbed floors. There was a young girl at a desk in the first office that McAvery introduced to me as Petra, Nava's daughter. We could see through into the other office that the sheriff was at his desk. Even sitting, the man was huge. He must have gone six or seven inches over six foot in height. What he might have weighed, I'd only guess for he was one of those big, raw boned men that can turnout to weigh fifty or sixty pounds more than your best guess.

He stood when he saw McAvery enter and came out to the front office. McAvery introduced me to him and after the banalties were over, I asked if we might go into his office on a fairly confidential matter. He invited me in and as I started to follow I noticed McAvery holding back.

"Come on my friend, you've earned the right to sit in on this meeting."

He smiled like a child on Christmas morning.

I started with the homesteaders being sent out with Johnson, the mineral rights filings and then told him of the filed deed of Clatilda's. I stopped there and asked the sheriff what he could do about the situation.

"Mr. Jackson, what's your connection with all of this?"

I told him I thought, just on the face of it, that the law should be able to take some action.

"Mr. Jackson, the only way I could do anything about this is if this Mrs. Bailey came in and signed a complaint. Then we might talk to Lawyer Johnson about several things; from claim jumping to outright theft of property. And when we got through with him . . . he might spend some time in front of a federal judge. It looks like he's cut it a little too close with this fooling around with those homesteaders."

I said nothing, just laid the Quit Claim Deed, putting the ranch in mine and Clatilda's names on his desk. He picked it up and read it through.

"Who's this Terry that notarized this deed? Is he that Mormon fellow that owns that general store?"

"That's him," I said.

"I know him slightly. He's a pretty good man. Honest as the day is long. Tell him I said hello."

"All right, But, now, does that deed change things?"

"You bet it does. You haven't filed it yet, have you?"

"No, I wanted to know more than I did before I filed it."

"Well, come on, that's the first order of business."

As we walked out, Nava told his daughter to tell anyone wanting to see him, he'd be around town. If they wanted him badly enough, to come find him. I'll swear he had to duck his head as we went through the door.

We went back to the County Clerk's office where I filed the deed. The woman there took out a printed Quit Claim deed and filled in the information from Clatilda's hand written one. She then wrote on it that it was a certified copy, signed, and stamped it with a huge seal. We took that copy and headed for Johnson's office. Nava told McAvery he might not want to come.

"Oh, yes he will!" I answered. "He's been too much help to miss the finish!"

Sheriff Nava grinned slightly and told McAvery to speak only when spoken to and to come on.

Johnson was not in his office but a sign on his door indicated he was out to dinner.

"That's no problem," McAvery said, "he takes his noon meal, every day down to the La Paloma Café"

"Well," said Nava, "let's go give this lawyer a little indigestion."

There was less than a half dozen people in the café. It was easy to pick out Johnson. He was the only one there wearing a suit. Nava walked right over to him and said, "Johnson, we've got business with you. Maybe we should step over to your office."

"I have regular office hours, sheriff. You want to see me, I'll be in my office after one o'clock this afternoon."

Nava stepped closer to the man, and while his voice was lowered, McAvery and I both heard.

"You have two choices, lawyer. Either we talk in your office or we talk here. For either choice, we get to talk right now!"

The man stood and glanced at all three of us.

"Nava, if this is not very important, I will make you regret interrupting my meal."

We made quite a parade, trooping back to Johnson's office.

After he had hung his coat and hat, Johnson sat behind his desk and looked at the sheriff.

"Get on with it, Nava. It's your show."

"Johnson, do you know the term 'claim jumping'?" Nava asked.

"Of course I do. I even know the legal term that applies in most mining states! What's that to do with me?"

"Well, I just thought you'd like to meet the fellow who, along with his wife, owns the ranch you've been filing mineral rights on."

"That can't be so!" said Johnson looking over at me.

"Why not, Johnson, did your people tell you I was dead?" I asked.

"No one told me anything. I just know that ranch is in an estate and it will be sometime before the courts get around to straightening it out. The widow filed a phony quit claim deed, but Mr. Bailey died intestate. That means he had no will. That property is in so much legal entanglement it could be years before it's straightened out."

"What about that, Jackson?" Nava said, turning to me.

"Well, sheriff, you know that Terry fellow you think so highly of?"

"Yeah, the one who's a notary."

"Yes, well he's the one who notarized that 'phony' quit claim deed Johnson is talking about, and on the date it shows, which is considerable earlier than Bailey's death."

"How would you know when Bailey died?" Johnson demanded.

"I just happened to have shot the bear that was killing him."

"Oh, and I guess you took real good care of the widow, too!" Johnson said.

Before Nava, McAvery or Johnson could even take a breath, I was standing against the front of Johnson's desk with my pistol barrel about two inches from his forehead, cocked.

"Friend, I've never heard of anyone timing how fast the hammer fell against the shell casing. But, that's how long you have to apologize to my wife."

"Put down that gun, cowboy, or I'll show you how long that takes?" said Nava from behind me.

"Sheriff, don't you know what will happen if you shoot me? Even should you touch me on the shoulder or hit me upside the head? I won't miss, and I'll guarantee this shyster will be dead. Back off! What's it to be, Johnson?"

"I'm sorry if I offended your wife. I apologize."

I holstered my pistol and stepped back so that Nava and McAvery were on my left.

"Arrest that man, sheriff, he just attempted to murder me!" said Johnson standing against his side of the desk.

"Now, let's just calm down here!" said Nava. "Do you claim, Johnson, that the quit claim from Bailey to his wife is illegal?"

"Of course it's illegal. You can tell by looking at it. It's just handwritten and as far as that notary, he's probably Mormon, and you know how those people will lie for one another!"

"Well, we'll just have to check that out, but in the meantime this man has just filed a deed on that ranch showing him and his wife as owners. You pursue this homesteading business and I'll have to lock you up for trespassing, and if this man finds even one flake of gold dust in that creek you've had your people homestead across, I'll lock you up for claim jumping. Furthermore, if you don't watch yourself, I'll send all this up to the federal judge in Denver, who handles homestead laws."

Johnson stood for a moment looking down at his desk. He then looked up at me.

"Jackson, there will continue to be people trying to homestead out there. Someday, there'll be one you won't be able to run off. That'll be the day I'll dance on your grave."

I looked over at Nava and McAvery. They were both staring at Johnson in slack-jawed amazement.

"Sheriff, how do you feel about fair fights in your town?" I asked.

"Fist fights or gunfights?"

"Gun fights."

"Well, cowboy, I sort of frown on them. Too many wild shots and one's liable to hit someone important to me. Now, was the fighters to go off, say, down by the stockyards, and as long as both men were armed, I guess I wouldn't have so much to say."

"Johnson, I'm sure you know where these stockyards are. I'll have to find out, but I'll be there in an hour. If you're not there, I'll see you branded for the coward you are!" I said.

I then turned and left Johnson's office, closely followed by Nava and McAvery.

As we were walking down the steps, I heard McAvery ask Nava if he thought Johnson would show up.

"Well, if he don't, he might as well spend the next hour packing. He won't be much good after failing to answer a fair challenge."

"Well, I'll just bet he doesn't. . ." McAvery was interrupted by two quick shots, one of which sent the sheriff's hat sailing out into the street.

McAvery jumped around the corner of the saddle maker's shop, and I turned drawing my pistol. I felt myself shoved over the stair rail to fall four or five feet to the ground. Before I hit the ground, I heard two shots then two more. I looked up to see Johnson fall against the landing rail then slump down and slide three or four steps down the staircase.

"Are you hurt?" Nava asked looking over the rail at me.

"No, did he get you?"

"No, but that back shooting snake just ruined my brand-new Stetson."

"Well, friend, I don't know what you think about taking gifts from strangers, but you come on over to the mercantile and I'll stand you to the best hat in the store."

"That won't even help!"

"Why not?" I asked.

"They don't carry one big enough for me. They have to order, all the way out of San Antonio!"

Both McAvery, who by now had stepped back out from the building, and I laughed.

"I'll get some folks to take care of this. And, Jackson, now, you're going to have to stay around for a day or two. There will be a coroner's inquest."

"Yeah, and while you're waiting, come on back to my place and we'll swap some more lies about prospecting," said McAvery.

I glanced sharply at him, but he was grinning wide.

The coroner's inquest was just a formality and lasted less than an hour, the day after the shooting.

As I was leaving town, I rode past the mercantile. I went in and paid the owner to order Nava the best hat he could get. I told him to tell Nava not to be hanging around with Mormon cowboys and jake-leg assayers. Maybe then he wouldn't get his hat ruined. He looked at me right funny but wrote down what I said. I paid him and left the store, got on my pony and headed home.

Like I've said before, there's nothing quite so pretty as a cabin in the mountains. Particularly if there's a family living in it. I had such a cabin and such a family in it. I did not dawdle.

Chapter 36

I felt good as I was riding across the San Luis valley toward home. It seemed the miles melted away as I rode toward my home and family. Outside of a brief rain shower in late afternoon, the trip was fine, and as dark began to catch up to me I knew my trip would soon be over.

When finally I topped over the mountain and started down the west side, I was pleased to see a faint light which I knew had to be our cabin. I was, somehow concerned and gigged my pony into a sharp trot. As I got closer, I could see the light to be a lantern hung outside the cabin door.

I was turning my horse into the barn when Clatilda came out of the cabin.

"When I heard the rider, I hoped it was you, Will. I half expected you yesterday, but I'm just glad you are finally here."

Arm in arm we went into the cabin which was warm, snug and smelling slightly of cinnamon.

"Lady, if you don't have an apple pie hidden somewhere, I'm going to be awfully disappointed."

Over our pie, I told Clatilda of the events of the past few days. She seemed dismayed about Johnson's death, in spite of all he had tried to do to us. I once again explained to her just how it had come about.

"Will, would you have faced Johnson in a gunfight if he had waited until you were both at the stockyards?"

"Yes, I thought to do just that. Can't you see, there was no other way?"I asked, watching to see her expression.

She said nothing, just turned to stare out at the moon appearing in one corner of the window. I could feel there was more she wished to say, so I kept silent.

"Will," she began, turning to face me, "we must talk about guns. I have thought and prayed much about this while you were gone, and I am afraid. I am afraid that someday I will have to see you placed beside Jennifer and Jethro."

When I started to respond, she reached across the table and placed her hand over mine.

"Will, please let me finish. I realize that your ability with guns and your willingness to use them has protected me and our ranch, but I worry that someday even your possession of a firearm might result in your injury or even your death."

"Clatilda, there is no way I can isolate myself from all danger. Why, I could be like Ted Branson, from down the valley, who had his horse stumble crossing the creek. Poor devil drowned before anyone could get to him. It's never possible to predict what might happen, particularly in the rough life we have chosen to live."

"Oh, Will, I know that's true, but carrying a gun and being quick to use it seems, to me, not in keeping with the Gospel."

"You should know by now that I will do all I can to live the Gospel, as far as I know and understand it. But will you tell me; of the few times, since I have been in this valley, that I have had to use a gun, which time would I have been better off to have been unarmed?"

She sat for a long moment with her eyes fixed and glazed while her mind seemed miles away. I kept my silence.

"I am as guilty as John Terry, and of the same thing!" she exclaimed, seeming to force herself out of her reverie. "I guess I was so concerned when you did not return when I thought you would. All I could imagine, as reason for your delay, was that you had been hurt or even killed."

"Clatilda, this is not like you. I've always felt you to be the strongest person, man or woman, I have ever met."

"Cowboy, I've always tried to be strong, but I guess I never felt I had so much to lose."

I will always remember that single statement as the finest homecoming of my life.

Chapter 37

(O)ur lives were without incident for the next few months and then our little Anna Laura was born. Or, as young Will called her, "Annie Lori." She arrived in the middle of torrential rain storm and cried enough that first week to match the amount of rainfall the night of her birth.

Of course, when Clatilda told me it was time, I went all to pieces and ran out of the cabin, almost tearing the barn door off its hinges. My horse must have thought me to be plumb crazy. It wasn't until I got to the Blalock's that I realized I should have brought a buggy or wagon. Seth and Annie both laughed at me and told me to go on back home, and they would be there shortly. I had barely put my horse away when Seth and Annie came rattling up in their light wagon. After we put Seth's team up and went into the cabin Annie exiled Seth and me to the kitchen with orders to be quiet and boil water. We boiled a lot of water, but I don't believe I remember any of it being used. Surely, I'm wrong.

Time drifted away as we ran our ranch and raised our children. Little Will began to be my constant companion. This fact pleased me very much. I found him a little pony, and Clatilda ordered him a small saddle through the store. He tickled me trying to make his fat little pony keep up with me on my horse. He had, somehow, developed the attitude that his contest was with my pony and not with me. On occasion I'd let him go ahead and then we would all hear about it at supper. That was about the only time he was ever very talkative.

For two years we sold our calf crops for top dollar. Clatilda wanted to keep part of each crop to increase the size of our herd but I told her of my plan to bring in four of the new short horn bulls to upgrade our herd. It was quite a day when Seth and I returned from Alamosa with our new bulls. Little Anna Laura somewhat took the wind from our sails, however. When she first saw them she turned to Clatilda and asked where Daddy had got such "litty-bitty cows."

Clatilda and Annie Blalock laughed until they had to go into the cabin leaving Will and Anna Laura watching Seth and I complete the corralling of the bulls. The thing about it was, when compared to our longhorns, the short horns did look rather small.

Seth and Annie also had two good years and on October fifteenth, in the middle of a howling blizzard, Seth handed Clatilda the final payment on their land. When we questioned them about coming out in such weather Seth answered saying that now that he could afford to pay back Clatilda's generosity, he wanted it done now so that come spring he might look at a little piece of land down-stream a couple of miles. His sly look and Annie's laugh took off the edge.

We had missed Sacrament services for two weeks due to the weather so it was in an almost festive air we prepared to leave that crisp November morning. It was cold; so cold the lines felt as sticks in my hands rather than straps of leather. As I breathed it felt as if my nostrils would stick together. The snow was soft and powdery and splashed from the horses' hooves like water.

We were almost halfway to town when I heard the sound of another wagon coming up behind us. I turned and looked back to see Seth, Annie and their three children pulling along beside us.

Thinking something amiss, I pulled my team to a stop and Seth did likewise.

"Is there anything wrong?" I asked.

"Nope," Seth answered. Just like that, no preamble, no explanation, just "nope."

"Well, then, where might you folks be off to on such a fine crisp morning?" I asked.

"Oh, we just thought to go into town to church," Annie answered.

For an instant I was about to say all right, then the folly of such a remark dawned on me.

"You do know there's only one church in town, don't you?" I asked.

"Yep." Seth responded as he slapped his reins against his team and moved out smartly ahead of us.

We spent an interesting time going on into town while speculating about what was going on in the Blalock family.

Clatilda commented that she didn't care what was going on, she was just glad to see them going to meetings.

I went on into the meeting house while Clatilda and the children sought out Annie and her brood. As I walked into the building, Bishop Terry, who was obviously waiting for me, shook my hand then guided me into the tiny room he called his office. When we sat down, he wanted to open our "meeting" with a prayer. I was curious but soon the prayer was over and then we sat and discussed several things including his questions about my support of the church authorities.

"I would say I probably do, Bishop," I responded, "but you and your counselors are the only 'authorities' I know"

"Brother Jackson," the Bishop said, leaning back in his chair, "among other things, the duties of the Church's General Authorities include the selection of a bishop, such as myself. I think it would be safe to say if you support me you sort of automatically support the General Authorities of our Church."

"Well, Bishop, when you put it that way, then I guess it's easy to support them."

We talked some more about the Church and how I helped in my way. Clatilda and I paid our tithes in two ways. I gave the best of our yearling stock each spring to the Bishop's storehouse, and Clatilda paid hers, on money received from the store, in cash.

Finally, Bishop Terry leaned back in his chair much as one who had completed a difficult task.

"Will, I imagine you're wondering why all the questions and, up until now, no answers. It is required that I interview each person who is to be called to some new station in the Church and prayerfully satisfy myself as to that person's worthiness. Having arrived at such a position I am prepared to issue a calling that you be ordained an elder in this Church. I have felt that for sometime the call should be made, but the recent decision of the Blalocks has forced the issue. You see, Seth and Annie, along with their oldest boy have asked to be baptized, and they have asked that you baptize them."

I almost fell out of my chair.

"Bishop Terry," I said, "I appreciate what you are doing as well as the Blalock's request but has everyone forgotten that it has been only a couple of years since you and your brother thought I should leave this country?"

"Somehow, Will, I don't believe the man John and I spoke to that day any longer exists," he responded.

"But, that's the point, Bishop. I may have been broke to halter but I will still protect the J-B and all of my family to the best of my ability and with any and every thing I can lay my hands on."

"Will, I know that I have, too often, questioned your activities and on at least one occasion misjudged your motives, but if you can forgive me, can I do less for you?"

"But, Bishop, you're a man of God. For me to forgive you is only right but suppose I once again have to protect my family with violence?"

"Pray that you are in the right, then get in touch with me, if you have time, and I'll see if I can't raise the 'Zion's Militia' again."

He then just sat there grinning at me like an indulgent father who'd just caught his favorite child with his hand in the cookie jar.

"Bishop, I've gotta believe you know what you're doing. At least I sure hope so."

"It's that simple, Will, you do what is right and Heavenly Father will take care of the rest. And, if you sincerely want to be his servant you will probably be surprised how well things will go for you and Clatilda and your children."

The Bishop briefly explained the ritual of ordination to me and said it would occur after Sacrament that evening. I walked from his office in a maze of conflicting thoughts. Believe me, my faith was sorely tested in that short walk from the Bishop's office to the meeting room. I was as frightened by the prospect of baptizing anyone as I had been at my own baptism. I did not doubt my own faith, I just felt really challenged that any one else would believe in it enough to allow me to introduce them into the Kingdom. When I entered the chapel, my first thought was to seek out Jess Turner. Finding him I sat down and began to lay out the whole thing. He chuckled and said he knew all about it, and he said he was right proud of me.

"You mean you are not just a little bit worried that I should be offered such a responsibility?" I asked.

"Let me ask you something, Will, are you more afraid of yourself or that the Blalocks may not be ready to be baptized?"

"Jess," I answered, "if Seth and Annie Blalock say they and their boy are ready to be baptized, you can take that statement to the bank and deposit it just as you would gold. Neither Seth nor Annie are given to taking responsibility lightly."

"What is your problem then, my friend?" Jess asked.

"I guess I'm just afraid I'll somehow mess up."

"After Priesthood is over you bring Clatilda and the kids to our house for dinner, and we'll teach you how it is all done."

When we got to the Turners, Hester met us at the door. She seemed very happy to see all of us. She and Clatilda were quickly involved in a conversation while Jess and I went into the parlor. Jess spent some time explaining both the mechanics and the spirit of the baptism. When we were both sure I had at least a fairly good grasp of the ritual, he asked me if I had been asked to do the confirmation of the Blalocks. I told him I didn't know as I had only been able to briefly congratulate Seth before the Bishop had whisked him away and into the Bishop's office right after Priesthood. He said that was all right, he would check with the Bishop and let me know right after sacrament.

I had thought to tell Clatilda about my new calling and the Blalock's baptism, but for some reason I felt it to be like blowing my own horn and had decided to wait until later. At the time I did not know what, if anything, Annie had told her.

At the dinner table Hester turned to Clatilda, "Well, how does it feel now that you have tamed this rapscallion to the point that he is to become an 'elder of Israel'?"

Clatilda's fork, raised halfway to her mouth, clattered loudly as it fell in her plate. She quickly turned to me, "Cowboy, did something happen this morning that you have forgotten to tell me?"

I still felt somewhat embarrassed to talk about it. All I could do was just nod.

Jess sat a little forward in his chair. "What's the matter, Will, don't you want to be an elder in your own church?"

"Absolutely, Jess! But to go around telling everyone seems an awful lot like bragging."

Jess looked at me for a moment, then leaned back in his chair. "Are you that happy to be called as an elder, son?"

"Well, I'll tell you Jess, outside of Clatilda and the children, it's the finest thing that has ever happened to me."

Clatilda rose and came around the table where I was sitting and quietly kissed my cheek, then returned to her seat. When everyone had settled down, Hester reached across the table and placed her hand over mine.

"Will," Hester said. "Please forgive me. I would not hurt you for anything. As you know, my mouth is frequently my worst enemy."

"Now there's an absolute fact!" chuckled Jess.

"Oh, be quiet, old man, I am talking to this good looking, young man here!"

Jess humphed and grumped but you could tell that Hester was the apple of his eye and as for her; I have no doubt she would charge the gates of hell with a teacup of water if she felt her Jess required or needed such to be done.

We sat around the Turner's table for almost an hour after dinner was finished and would have tarried longer, but it became time to leave for Sacrament meeting.

That afternoon, at Sacrament, Bishop Terry presented me to the membership and announced that the ordination would take place in his office, right after the meeting. He was wrong. The number of people that showed up required we go back to the chapel. By the time we got away from the meeting house my right hand was almost numb. I don't ever remember shaking so many hands, even at our wedding.

I was quiet as we went home in the cold clear night, but I did think to ask Clatilda what she thought about the Blalock's baptism. She spun around on the wagon seat, to face me.

"So that's what all the secrecy is about!" She exclaimed.

She then told me about how Annie had refused to give her any good reason why they were attending the meeting, except to say Clatilda would know all about it soon enough. It was not until I had put the animals in their stalls and milked the cow and the pair of goats that were fresh that I felt like discussing the days events with Clatilda. Our discussion was not long and would have concluded with her comment that she was glad to have the full benefit of the priesthood in her home, but I asked her if Jethro had not held the priesthood. That question seemed to go all the way down the well and back. She finally responded that he had the priesthood, but it had benefitted "their" home. And now she had the priesthood in "her" home. She seemed to put a lot of stock in the difference.

The morning after that eventful Sabbath I milked and fed the stock, and after hitching up the buckboard, my brood and I went up to the Blalocks. After the welcomes and congratulations, it was agreed the Blalocks would be baptized the last Thursday in November. We stayed for a late breakfast, or early dinner, whichever. All I know is, it was delicious. After we had eaten, I turned to Seth.

"Tell me something, Seth, after the hassles you and I have had, why did you and Annie ask me to baptize you and your family?"

"Well, I'll tell you, Will, among the people we know that have never, ever lied to us at one time or another, you and Clatilda stand at the head of the list. Naturally Clatilda was our first choice, but the Bishop said she wasn't allowed so we just had to settle for you." Even while he was still talking, a grin spread across his face.

"Seth Blalock, you ought to be ashamed of yourself!" Annie said as she reached over and slapped him on the shoulder.

Clatilda told Seth she agreed that while he was probably right about me being a poor second choice, sometimes you just had to make do with whatever was at hand.

I looked around the table and leaned back in my chair. I reckoned as how it was unusually warm, and nice, to be in the midst of such good fellowship.

Thus, was a fine morning whiled away until it was long after dinner by the time I got the team and buckboard put away. Clatilda met me at the door and swung her arms around my neck.

"I got me a cowboy with a sense of humor and one who is going to have a bigger family than he had ever thought he would."

It took a moment for that last to sink in. The only thing I could think of to ask was, when?

"Late May, probably; maybe early June."

I rode down to the stack-yard that afternoon to open the gate to another hay stack for our herd. It dawned on me that I would soon be responsible for four people, in addition to myself. The thought of such responsibility was staggering to a Panhandle cowboy. I then began to see that the responsibility was not mine alone. At first I had trouble even thinking about such a possibility. The more I thought, the more comforted I became. It was not just the help I received from the men in our ward, but more, much more. That afternoon standing in that high mountain valley, I think I finally, truly, understood what Clatilda always called "The Gospel."

I prayed and did so with a gentle expectancy of having my prayers answered. I thought about my newfound confidence until it dawned on me that I might not always like the answer I got from my prayers. I believe it was at that instant that I gained my testimony of the truthfulness of the Gospel. I rode off, heading back to the cabin and my family to tell them of my new found truth.

This time there was no shyness or concern about blowing my own horn. I was ready to shout it from the highest mountain. I stopped there for a moment and had myself a good laugh. The humor in the idea of the Panhandle cowboy of a few years ago, shouting his belief in the Gospel from a mountain could be best appreciated by another Panhandle cowboy, possibly Hester Turner and definitely

Clatilda Jackson.

As I rode on toward my mountain cabin, I got to thinking about my first evening up on the mountainside looking down into the valley just before the bear had killed Jethro Bailey. I could remember my loneliness of that evening but could find no such emotion in me now. This was a joy I would carry in my heart to my grave.